THE SHORT LIST

ALSO BY ERIC BEETNER & FRANK ZAFIRO

The List Series
The Backlist

ALSO BY ERIC BEETNER

Leadfoot
When the Devil Comes to Call
The Devil Doesn't Want Me
Rumrunners
The Year I Died Seven Times
Run for the Money (previously *Criminal Economics*)
Dig Two Graves
White Hot Pistol
Stripper Pole at the End of the World
A Bouquet of Bullets (stories)
Fightcard: Split Decision
Fightcard: A Mouth Full of Blood

With JB Kohl
Over Their Heads
Borrowed Trouble
One Too Many Blows to the Head

ALSO BY FRANK ZAFIRO

River City Series
Under a Raging Moon
Heroes Often Fail
Beneath a Weeping Sky
And Every Man Has to Die

Stefan Kopriva Mysteries
Waist Deep
Lovely, Dark, and Deep
Friends of the Departed

Ania Trilogy (with Jim Wilsky)
Blood on Blood
Queen of Diamonds
Closing the Circle

Some Degree of Murder (with Colin Conway)
At Their Own Game
The Last Horseman
At This Point in My Life
Chisolm's Debt
The Trade Off (with Bonnie Paulson)

To Dad & Gail —
With love, as always!

ERIC BEETNER &
FRANK ZAFIRO

THE SHORT LIST

DOWN & OUT
BOOKS

Down & Out Books
3959 Van Dyke Rd, Ste. 265
Lutz, FL 33558
www.DownAndOutBooks.com

Cover design by JT Lindroos

ISBN: 1-943402-28-0
ISBN-13: 978-1-943402-28-1

To my Boston life: the lousy apartments, the hardcore shows at the Rat, long walks through history, rooftops on Beacon Hill and four of the best (and coldest) years of my life.

—Eric

For my friend, Dave Mather. Thanks for bringing me along.

—Frank

"I have just returned from Boston. It's the only sane thing to do if you find yourself up there."
—Fred Allen in a letter to Groucho Marx

"Revenge is an act of passion; vengeance of justice. Injuries are revenged; crimes are avenged."
—Samuel Johnson

ONE
Cameron

Time never moves slower than when the guy you're supposed to kill is late to the appointment for his own death. So I sat in the corner table listening to yet another forgotten hit of the seventies and eighties and took baby sips on my beer. Couldn't get sloppy on a job night.

I kept my eyes on the door and on Bricks as she sat at the bar, empty stool beside her. Every time someone would come up and try to sit she'd say she was waiting for a friend or that her girlfriend was in the bathroom. If this guy didn't show soon the people standing at the bar top elbowing in for drinks were gonna start to get pissed.

It had been more than nine months since Bricks and I began working together, about the length of a pregnancy and our little murder-for-hire business was about to be delivered a stillborn. Yeah, business was slow.

Since our blood-soaked exit from the family, she and I thought there would be a ton of work mopping up the turf war between the New England factions and the Florida douchebags intent on squashing them. Not so much. We seemed to have done such a good job of beheading the New York office that very little stood in the way of a Florida takeover and, brother, they invaded like a swarm of those big flying palmetto bugs they got down there.

We took the occasional cheating spouse job, two corporate jobs—Wall Street, of course—and a whole lot of nothing. This jackass about to arrive at the bar would be maybe the last step between us hanging up our gun belts or staying locked and loaded for the next call to come in.

We even took our show on the road for this one. Boston. A good town, if you can deal with the most obnoxious sports fans this side of Philadelphia. Or if you can get past the accent. Give me a good dose of Brooklyn or Staten Island twang any day over the dropped Rs and nasally whine.

This guy was in international finance. A real piece of work. Swiss, I think. At least he was in town on business from Switzerland. He had a long list of fetishes and sexual deviances, so the way to set him up was through his crotch, which led to Bricks and me working as a team for the first time. Usually when we got a client we would split it up. One person would help with the legwork and setting up the how and where of a hit, but we'd let one of us alone go do the job. We'd both come from a solo career and that's where we felt comfortable. At least, I did. I think Bricks wanted to stay out of my line of fire, to be honest. I had a history of, shall we say, jobs that required cleanup. I'd been much better since she and I went into business together. Maybe the old gal was rubbing off on me.

So the setup was this: Bricks parks herself at this swanky Copley Square bar right next to the hotel where Mr. Swiss is staying. We got here a few days early and noticed he stops in almost every night for a few drinks before heading to bed, usually with the intent on finding a woman to bring upstairs with him. He was batting zero from what we'd witnessed. This was good for us. He'd be horny.

Look, I've grown to love Bricks like a sister, but Paula

Brickey is not a traditional beauty. She'd tell you the same. But for this horny Swiss bastard, all we needed her to be was available.

At first she was definitely not excited about the plan, but she came around when we both realized it was our best bet to get him away from a crowd. She was sitting at the bar like a spider perched on the edge of a freshly made web. All we needed was for him to walk into it and get trapped. See, Mr. Swiss had a thing for dressing in women's underpants—I'm telling you, the file on this guy read like soft core porn—so all Bricks has to do is flirt like hell with the guy, convince him she'll come up to his room with him but only after he slips on a pair of her panties. She hands him a pair she's already got stashed in her bag and when he goes to the john to change, I follow him in and...

One more job down and hopefully we've got a repeat client.

A waitress came by and asked me if I wanted another beer. I waved her off, showing her the two fingers of pale ale still in my bottle. She didn't look pleased and who could blame her. Probably a college girl living off her tips, and slow drinkers are lousy tippers by nature.

The conversation level was giving me a headache, along with the shrill synthesizer noises on the latest one hit wonder from the 1980s. This was the kind of bar I'd normally never be caught dead in, but it was good enough to make someone dead in, I supposed.

Foursomes and sextets of twenty-something weeknight drinkers seemed to go out of their way to announce to the whole place what a great goddamn time they were having by laughing like they were drinking with George Carlin. A group of guys in the corner with matching Red Sox hats made it sound like there were in a contest with each other for who could laugh the loudest. If this Swiss guy didn't show soon I was still gonna get my kill that night. If those overgrown fraternity assholes only knew.

I checked the door and checked Bricks. She gave me a subtle over-the-shoulder look and made her eyes go wide in frustration. If he didn't show in the next ten minutes I'd call it and we could come back tomorrow night. Maybe he'd already found a willing slut to take back to his room so she could spank him and call him Shirley or whatever sick bastard shit he was into.

But another night meant another hotel for me and Bricks. The payday on this job was good, but not knowing when the next gig was coming made us both a little tightfisted when it came to the bank accounts.

I decided *fuck it* and downed the last swallow of my beer and looked around for the college girl to get me another. Mr. Swiss walked in the door. One of the frat boys told another whopper and the laughter nearly drowned out Rick Springfield's lament for Jessie's girl.

I wiped my palms on my pants when I realized they'd suddenly gone sweaty. Game on. I was ready for my part. Now it was Bricks' turn to snag him in that web of hers.

TWO
Bricks

A honey trap. That is the last con I ever imagined I'd play a part in. Those kind of gigs usually involve some slutty siren who drips sex appeal. About the only thing I ever drip is sweat from a hard aikido workout.

But I am a woman, and damnit, every woman can be sexy, right?

Right?

We'd see.

The Swiss answer to sexual deviancy stood near the door, scanning the room. I glanced at Cam to make sure he'd seen our mark, then turned away, managing to flip my hair in the process. I'd been letting it grow and now that my curls reached shoulder length, they actually did something when I flipped my hair.

Which was never.

At least I didn't have to giggle at the same time, or croon the blonde mating call, "Oh my God, I'm sooooo drunk!"

The stool next to me was the only one along the entire bar that was still open, so it wasn't like Swiss Boy Robinson had much of a choice. True to form, he appeared at my shoulder less than a minute later.

"Is someone sitting here?" he asked me. His accent was thick and haughty, though I'm sure he thought it was slick and hottie. I gave him a bored look over my shoulder, then hesitated just long enough to let a little interest seep into my expression. When I was pretty sure he'd noticed, I dropped the disinterested mask back into place.

"If he is, he's invisible," I said.

A touch of a smile tugged at the corners of his mouth. "Ah, a touch of New York, here in Boston. How cosmopolitan." He sat down on the chair next to me and signaled the bartender.

I'd already decided that the hard ass, hard to get mistress was the card to play with this guy, but his comment gave me an excuse to continue the conversation while staying in character. Besides, I was a little curious how he'd pegged my accent. "How'd you know I was New York?"

"Your accent, of course."

"I don't have an accent."

"But you do. And it is very definitely a New York accent."

The bartender appeared in front of us, looking at him expectantly.

"I will have an old fashioned, bitte."

The bartender scrunched his brow. "You want it bitter?"

"No, I'm sorry. Just a standard old fashioned. And please bring the lady another of whatever she is having."

I held up my half-full glass of red wine. "Vino. House."

The bartender nodded and was gone.

I gave our man a sardonic look. "You get on my accent, but at least I came in here speaking English, pal."

"Is that what they speak here in Boston?" He shook his head. "Well, if it qualifies as English, it is only as a regional dialect."

"You sure you're not British? That sounds like something a Brit would say, all pissed off at what we Americans have done to his mother tongue."

"And where do you suppose they stole most of that mother tongue? From Deutsch."

"From the Dutch?"

He smiled indulgently, then leaned in towards me conspiratorially. "Let's not pretend that you are a stupid woman, or that I would be interested in any such thing. I believe we will get along much better if we do so."

"Who says I'm pretending? Maybe I'm just breaking your balls."

His smile widened. "A curious expression. Very American. I rather like it, though I wish it had a different meaning."

"Like?"

"Something not quite so painful."

I took a slow sip of my wine, thinking. I'd hoped to charm him with the gritty, hard to get angle. Being the femme fatale wasn't in my wheelhouse. But my pops always told me to follow my gut, and that not to was a big mistake. Where he came from, and where I grew up, there are some mistakes you don't come back from.

So I shifted into unfamiliar territory. I eyed him up and down and took another sip. That gave the bartender time to return with our drinks. My new friend ignored his while I polished off the rest of my glass of wine and placed it next to the full one he'd bought for me. I made sure to leave some lipstick on the rim for good measure, as I tapped my fingernail on the glass.

"You're very forward," I said from low in my throat. I was hoping for a husky growl, something along the lines of Mae West, but it came out sounding more like Kathleen Turner with a cold.

"Yes. But I'm afraid I must be. You see, I am only here for this final evening before I return home."

"Where's home, exactly?"

"Dusseldorf."

"Is that in Switzerland?"

His eyes narrowed. "No, of course not. It is in Germany."

Shit.

I reached for my wine glass. "Oh, I though you sounded Swiss. They speak German, too, right?"

He contemplated me for a long uncomfortable moment. I drank some vino and gave him a look with just a hint of smolder in it. At least, that was what I was shooting for. If I had the same luck as my Mae West voice, I probably just looked like I was constipated.

His expression softened, though, and he picked up his drink, took a gentlemanly swallow, and smiled. "The Swiss cannot choose a side in war, politics, or business. Nor can they choose a language. They speak German, true, but also French and Italian. Really, all they are good for is making watches and banking. Especially banking."

"And chocolate."

"German chocolate is far superior."

I made a pouty smile. "I'll bet."

"One might argue we are better at banking, too. The bank I work for is a particular example." He took another drink, this one much longer. When he set the glass down, it was almost empty. "Tell me, what is your name?"

"Bella," I told him.

"Bella," he mused. "How appropriate."

I smiled at him, but all I could think was spare me.

"Bella, I am Konrad."

I held out my left hand like a debutante. "Charmed."

He took it lightly, and then the bratwurst brain actually kissed my knuckle. I knew Cam was watching this, and that I'd never hear then end of this bullshit. But I smiled and acted impressed.

We sat there for another twenty minutes, though if you'd asked me at the time, I'd have said it was two hours. Or two years. As urbane and European as Konrad purported to be—and truth be told, his manners fit the bill—in the end, he was just another horny guy looking to get his rocks off. Just another man who thinks the most interesting conversation is one in which he talks about himself, or what he thinks, or what he plans to accomplish.

Only this one happened to piss off the wrong people. With some cash to spend. And the right number to call.

It took him most of that twenty minutes to make himself believe he'd wowed me with his sophistication. I'm sure he thought he had me so primed I was about ready to slide right off of my chair. Of course, I had something to do with that perception. I played up the sexy almost-vamp, throwing in the occasional innuendo to lead him down the garden path.

By the time we'd worked ourselves into talking about fantasies, I was really glad that Cam was going to handle this one. He had a penchant for the messy, and Konrad the douchebag Deuatscher deserved it based on self-image alone.

"I find traveling is a great opportunity to explore one's

boundaries," he told me right after we broke the ice on fantasies.

"I've found it is the very best opportunity," I added.

"And what boundaries do you wish to explore, mein Bella?"

"Why? Are you looking to be my Marco Polo?"

"I am."

I glanced around surreptitiously. "And are you willing to do whatever I say?"

"Oh, almost certainly."

"Because I don't figure you European guys are as hung up on some things as most Americans. You can probably do what I want you to do without feeling like it's weird."

He smiled perhaps his first genuine smile of the night. "I believe I am able to guarantee that."

I gave him a look that was meant to be half seductive, half conspiratorial. Then I reached for my purse, popped it open and showed him the lace edge of a pair of black panties. "I want you to put these on and meet me in my room," I whispered, staring directly into his eyes. "Will you do that for me, Konrad?"

He didn't answer, but the lust brewing in his bright blue windows to the soul told me I'd hit it out of the park. He'd climb a razor blade pole to get to me now.

I balled the panties up into my palm, then pressed them against his stomach. For all his outward appearances of calm but lustful, touching him told me a different story. Heat radiated off of his body, and I could feel his heartbeat tripping along.

He covered my hand with his own, then took the panties and placed them in his jacket pocket. His eyes never left mine. I gave him my best intense "fuck me" look, striving for an Oscar. Meanwhile, my stomach turned at what he must be thinking.

"Allow me to finish my drink?" he said softly.

I shook my head. "We'll order room service."

He didn't hesitate. "Very well." He removed his billfold and laid a fifty dollar bill on the bar. "Will you wait here?"

"No. I'll be in my room. Waiting."

"Which room?"

"Nine Oh Four. Knock just once."

He nodded, all business now that he'd landed me. He left his chair and strode confidently away without a backwards glance.

I caught Cam's eye from across the room and nodded after Konrad, who was all but goose-stepping his way to the men's room. The panty routine was more than just to get him hot and bothered, it was to keep him in that bathroom stall for a while and make Cam's job easier.

Me, I stood up and walked out of that bar as Konrad hit the bathroom door.

Needless to say, I wasn't staying at the hotel. I picked the room number because it was Mike Richter's career save percentage. I wasn't huge into hockey but my pops was still around in '94 when the Rangers won the Cup, and he'd been pretty excited. He told me that everyone said it was Messier, the team captain, who was the reason for the win, but Pops always said it was the goalie the whole way. He never quit on a play, Pops said. Plus he was an American-born player in a league full of Canadians, so he had that going for him, too.

I breezed through the lobby of the hotel, and out the front door. There weren't any cabs lined up outside, but I saw one half a block over and hailed it with a hearty whistle. And maybe I stuck my leg out, too. Just a little.

The cabbie pulled up to a stop. I got in back, but left the door open. "Start the meter, but I'm waiting for someone."

"Sure thing, doll." He smiled at me in the rearview mirror, his coffee-stained teeth looking yellow in the reflection of the streetlights.

Doll?

Normally, that would piss me off, but tonight was different. It was a strange night, and I was feeling it. Playing the sex kitten was actually a little bit...fun. And I might not be any threat to the legacy of Angelina Jolie, but I was a woman. And every woman can be sexy, right?

You're fucking right.

THREE
Cameron

As soon as I saw him slide off the bar stool, I jumped up to beat him to the men's room. I banged the table with my knee, knocked over my brand new beer. A trio of co-workers at the table next to me stopped their conversation and gave me annoyed over-the-shoulder stares, but I didn't have time to apologize. I had a man to kill.

I must have looked like I had the runs while I hot-footed it to the bathroom. I got there only a few steps ahead of Mr. Swiss, but he got held up in the short hallway outside the john by a pair of backslapping ex-frat types. It gave me just enough cushion.

In the bathroom were two stalls, two urinals and two sinks. No people. So far, so good.

I knew he had to go into a stall to change into the underpants, all part of the plan. So I ducked into the first stall and shut the door. In my jacket pocket was the wire. A palm-sized wooden handle on each end, piano wire stretched between. I always wondered what note that string played, but I'd never found out.

I unspooled the garrote and gripped it in both hands. A public place like this was fraught with way too many dangers. Trying to get away after gunshots was simply not on the list of smart options. So a silent kill was necessary. I wondered if we weren't so hard up for cash if I'd take the same risks this job proposed.

Soon after I had the weapon in both hands I heard the

door open, the music getting momentarily louder and then being muffled again. The band playing over the speakers was Boston. Being played in the city of Boston. Weird. The last song this guy would ever hear.

I followed the sound of his footsteps on the tile as he passed by my stall and entered the open one next to me. I heard his belt unbuckle, pants drop. All normal bathroom sounds.

I gave him a second more, then put a foot up on the toilet, no lid, only a U-shaped seat. Kicking in the door to his stall was an approach I'd considered, but it was loud, would make the space cramped, and then left the kill on view for the next visitor when the job was done. To get to him while the door was still locked meant he wouldn't be found until the cleaning crew after last call.

I raised up slowly and peeked over the top, my feet balancing on the plastic toilet seat. From what I knew about this guy, he'd probably like being spied on while he dressed in women's panties. If there was a glory hole between these two stalls, I bet I could get him to blow me.

I saw the top of his head and a pronounced bald spot. There was a ring of sweat stain on the back collar of his white shirt. His head was down as he pulled on the lace number Bricks had given him. I reached over with the loop of wire and aimed it at his neck.

As the thin piano string passed in front of his eyes his head jerked up and I yanked. Before he could turn his head up and see me, I had him in a noose of metal. I pulled hard, getting my elbows up to the top of the wall between stalls. He was thrashing now, his legs kicking in stunted half-kicks since the panties were around his ankles.

His fingers dug at his neck, searching for the wire and an inch of space he could wedge himself into to ease the pressure, but there was none to be found. The wire dug deep in the folds of his neck, swallowed by flesh and starting to cut. I gave an upward jerk, sweat forming on my face as I grimaced with the effort. I realized I had been holding my breath and I let out a loud exhale. Only after I did it did I realize what a mocking gesture it was—loudly showing off all the air I could get in and out of my lungs.

His elbows banged the metal walls between our cubicles. Sputters of the last air in his throat and mouth burst out. Then I was falling.

My foot was wet. My wrist screamed in pain. I'd let one foot slide off the toilet seat and land in the bowl. My right arm was stretched out, my wrist painfully wrenched over the top of the stall as I held onto the loop of wire for dear life—and to end his.

I lifted my foot out, only to have my other foot splash in its place. Looking down I could see in the gap under the stalls that his feet had left the ground. My body weight falling had lifted him.

I rescued my other foot and had to step down onto the floor to reposition myself. My arms ached as I strained to keep hold of the garrote. Blood began pouring to the floor on his side of the wall. The wire had broken through.

The Swiss man's struggles stopped almost immediately. The blood came down quickly, like he was pissing away a night's worth of beer and missing the bowl.

I stood on the toilet seat again, easing up for a second on the wire. His body slipped and his feet touched ground. By the time I stood tall and tightened my grip again I realized I was holding dead weight.

I didn't hear the door open, but the music got louder. "More Than a Feeling."

"Hold on, I gotta take a wicked piss."

So I knew he was a local. Good news was he sounded alone. I slid as far back to the tiled wall of the bathroom as I could to keep my arms draped over the divider out of sight from the man headed for a urinal. I didn't want to let the Swiss man drop. The sound would be a giveaway, plus he might slip a leg out from under the stall door or something.

The muscles in my forearms burned. First from the strangulation, now the holding of a two-hundred-pound carcass of prime Swiss meat. Sweat dripped into my eyes but my hands were clawed onto the wooden handles of the wire loop and couldn't help me.

Piss hit the porcelain basin of the urinal outside the stalls, and this was indeed a wicked one. He kept going and going like he hadn't seen a bathroom in a week.

I grunted. Couldn't help it. Still, not entirely out of place sound in a toilet stall.

The fountain of urine outside continued to fall.

My foot slipped again. I splashed into the bowl a third time. He had to have heard it, even over the sounds of his racehorse piss.

"Jesus, buddy," he said. The beer might've been leaving his body, but it had already made its way to his brain. He sounded drunk and had to laugh at me.

"Don't get the chowder," I said, though I skipped trying to do the accent—chowdah. He laughed at that too, then started to wrap things up quickly, I assumed to head off the massive cloud of stink he thought would soon be emanating from my stall. Score one for my slippery foot.

He set off the flusher and left the room without washing his hands, and for that I was grateful. As soon as the music settled back into the pillow-over-the-ears muffle, I let the Swiss man fall. The sound of his body collapsing, banging against the toilet bowl, echoed off the tile and mirror walls.

I sat down on the toilet and panted for breath. My hands were frozen in a claw-fingered grip. I'd let one side of the wire loose and the other end dangled from my left hand, the wire slick with blood. On the tile floor between the stalls the pool of blood had found its way to the drain set in an indent in the floor, there to catch piss from those too drunk to aim well.

I bent down and gave his legs a shove, pushing his body into the stall so no part of him hung out. I evaluated my work. Not good enough. If someone bent down to look, they'd see him in a heap. Probably see the blood too.

I took off my jacket and hung it on the little hook there. First time in my life, I think, I'd ever used one of those things. I got down on the floor and slid under, hurrying since I knew there was more than one guy in the bar with a wicked piss in him.

My shirt got streaked with blood as I passed from one stall to the other. Fresh blood was probably not the worst thing my shirt picked up under there. Working fast I got him seated on the toilet and balanced so he'd stay. Up close, I saw the damage my wire had done. A ragged line was torn across his neck, blood and strings of flesh like the torn hem of a garment. His eyes were a maze of burst blood vessels, his tongue swollen and purple, wouldn't fit in his mouth. Worst of it all were the little black panties he wore.

I slid back under, coating more of my shirt in blood and urine, who knows what else. The door opened again just as I got under into my own stall. I stood, wiped sweat off my forehead with a wad of toilet paper, and pulled my jacket on over my bloodstained shirt.

I unlocked the stall door and almost forgot to flush. Gotta keep up the illusion.

I, too, left without washing my hands.

Outside I found Bricks waiting in a cab, as planned. I slid in next to her and it took her a second to realize all had not gone smoothly.

"What the—"

"Don't ask," I said.

FOUR
Bricks

I made it through the cab ride back to our hotel without a word. Cam was fidgety next to me, but I'd gotten to know him well enough to know what kind of fidget it was. He had a few. There was the *worried about the business* fidget, which involved pacing and lots of talking. His *pre-game* fidget was actually pretty minimal, usually just a little bit of knee twitching and silence. Of course, I was very familiar with the *Tia* fidget, which was all over the map, but always included biting his upper lip. I've grown attached to the guy, but the way he frets about that girlfriend of his? Crazy.

This kind of fidgeting fit none of the above, though. And it wasn't the euphoric, triumphant, *we are so bad-ass* reaction he sometimes had when we finished a job. I hadn't seen this one in a while. Not since our ad hoc partnership started, when it was the first of his idiosyncrasies that I learned.

No, this one was his *I fucked up* fidget.

I casually looked him over during the cab ride. I didn't see any obvious injuries on his face or hands. I couldn't see any blood on his clothing, either, but his shoes were sopping wet.

What the hell? Did he dance in the fucking toilets or what?

I kept my mouth closed. At the hotel, I paid the cab driver, along with enough of a tip to make him happy but not remember us. Once we stepped onto the curb, Cam headed straight for the front door of the hotel. I caught up to him as he entered the lobby and snaked my arm around his.

"Let's hit the bar," I said.

His eyes widened in surprise, and he glanced down at where our arms were linked. "Uh...Bricks, I...I, uh, don't know if..."

I scowled. Seriously, does every man's first thought go to sex?

Stupid question.

"For Christ's sake, relax," I told him. "I just want to talk."

"Oh." He gave me a weak, worried grin.

I ignored him and strode through the door to the lounge. Without a word, I guided us to a table in the corner and nudged him toward the chair. Then I flopped into the seat with my back to the wall. The bartender wasn't busy but he seemed oblivious to us.

I took off my jacket and motioned for Cam to do the same. I didn't want him thinking this was going to end in five minutes. We were going to be there long enough to have a drink and talk.

He shook his head.

"Cam? Lose the jacket."

Head shake, a little more forcefully.

"What is this Seinfeld shit? Take off your jacket and stay a few minutes. Christ."

He shook his head again.

"Suit yourself," I muttered. I rooted around in my purse for a tissue but couldn't find one. I used the napkin wrapped around my silverware to wipe the whorish shade of lipstick off. I could feel Cam watching me. His nervous tension hadn't dissipated. I balled up the napkin and gave him an even stare. "You want to tell me what happened?"

He looked down at the table and sighed. Then he looked back up at me. "I did the job, Bricks. Swiss Man is dead. We're getting paid."

"He was German."

"What?"

"The target. He was—"

"Something to drink?" A waiter appeared to my left and I'd been so focused on Cam that I didn't see him approach and was surprised. My immediate inclination was to put him into a wrist lock and take him to his knees but I resisted. He was just a waiter, after all, and I was mad.

"Two beers," Cam ordered. "Whatever light you have on draft."

The waiter slinked away, and now I was irritated with Cam for ordering for me.

I took a deep breath.

Stop acting like a chick.

Cam was about to say something but I held up my hand to stop him. "You want to explain why you're acting like you just did a rehash of Slaughterhouse?"

His face fell at the nickname. "It...it wasn't like that."

"Yes, it was. I know your fidgets."

"My what?"

I waved off his question. "Spill."

He glanced left and right for anyone nearby, then leaned in. "Like I said, I took care of it. The Swiss guy—"

"German, I said."

He gave me an odd look. "How do you know that?"

"I sat with Mr. Sauerkraut for half an hour, listening to his bullshit. He's from Dusseldorf."

He stared at me. "Okaaaaaay. Swiss, German, why does that matter?"

I pushed up the sleeve of my blouse, showing him the marbled scars on my left forearm. "That's why."

He stared at the scar tissue for a little while. That irritated me, too, so I dropped my arm and pushed the sleeve forward again.

Jesus. Did anything not rub me wrong tonight?

"Which one was that?" Cam asked me quietly. His voice had a little boy quality to it, one that was genuine and unpretentious. Kinda sweet. It reminded me that I liked the guy. That he was a friend, which was something I didn't have many of.

Try none, if I'm being honest.

And Cam was more than a friend. He wasn't quite like a little brother, though I felt that way about him sometimes. Mostly, he was a good partner.

And I was being a bitch.

"Tommy Davenport," I said, not meeting his gaze at first. Then I looked up at him. "He had a dog, pit bull with no vocal cords."

He gaped. "What the hell for?"

"I'm not sure. He was guarding a stash. Or a bank, more likely. It doesn't matter. The important part is this." I waited a beat for emphasis, then said, "I walked into a situation with shit intel, and what happened was that things went to shit. That was no coincidence."

He nodded slowly, then stopped. "Wait. So you're saying things went to shit on this one? Or that they went to shit because the Swiss guy was German?"

"Neither. I'm saying I can tell something happened in the bathroom because you're acting like Slaughterhouse over here. And I'm saying that details matter. We've got to stay on top of the intel, or things can go sideways. Will go sideways."

Cam was silent for a while. The waiter arrived with our beers and he turned his glass on the table without drinking any of it. He just stared into the amber liquid, his face somber. Finally, he sighed and shrugged. "What can I say, Bricks? Some guys are good at sports, some are lucky at cards, and some guys get the babes. Me? I get the job done, and it always gets messy."

"That what happened in the bathroom?"

"Yeah, kinda."

"How?"

"He bled a lot. That's why I kept my jacket on. I got blood on my shirt."

"How much?"

"Streaks, I think. It's on my back."

"On your back? What the hell?"

So he told me the story. How the garrote cut deep. How Konrad from Dusseldorf bled like a stuck schwein. Holding up the dead weight while some Southie took a "wicked piss." And then going under the stall to prop Konrad up on the toilet.

He told the whole thing without touching his beer, and I listened without touching mine.

"I really need a shower," he said when he'd finished.

"And we gotta lose those clothes."

He raised an eyebrow. "You keep hitting on me, partner, and I'm either going to take you up on it or file sexual harassment charges."

"Cut it," I said. "You aren't suave enough to pull off a line like that. Besides, you're not my type."

I caught another look from him before he looked down at the beer in front of him. It was the loud question that occasionally popped up in our friendship but went unasked. Which was good, because I wasn't answering it. The last person to ask me about my love life was Bruno Taggliarti, one of Don Giordano's thugs. He was obsessed about whether I liked men or women and took every opportunity to be obnoxious about it. He was obnoxious about everything else, too, but especially that.

He stopped being obnoxious, though. For good.

Regarding his fixation, though, my thought on the matter was simple. Whose business was it? And in the grand scheme of things, why did it matter?

But it seemed to matter to some people. More than it should. And I knew Cam wanted to ask, but he also knew better than to do so. It's not that I feel particularly secretive about that part of my life. It's that I feel particularly secretive about all of my life. Yeah, Cam was part of that life, but he was on a need to know basis. For that matter, he didn't know what I named the cactus I bought last week, either.

Like I said, a need to know basis.

I let the awkward moment pass. That was the nice thing about Cam. There were sometimes awkward moments, but they all passed pretty quickly.

Cam sat glumly staring into his beer again. Telling the story seemed to have brought him down. I reached for my beer and raised it in a toast. "To finishing the job."

He hesitated, then picked up his own glass and reluctantly clinked mine. I drank. He didn't.

I gave him a hard stare.

He sighed and took a swig. After he swallowed, he added, "Only to make you happy."

"I don't know why you're down all of the sudden. You seemed pretty proud of yourself when we sat down."

"That was before you pointed out to me how much I *Slaughterhoused* the whole thing."

"I didn't say that. I said you were acting like you did." I took another drink. The beer tasted surprisingly good. "Anyway, it sounds to me like things went stellar."

His face brightened a little, cautiously. "Really?"

I nodded. "Really. Listen, there's an old saying my pops used to tell me. 'No battle plan survives contact with the enemy.' You've probably heard it, right?"

"Yeah. I think Norman Schwarzkopf said it or something."

"He may have said it. A lot of people have repeated a version of it, but you'll like this. The guy who originally said it was a German general." Then I added, "Probably from Dusseldorf."

He chuckled ruefully. "That's awesome."

"Yeah. There's another saying, too, that my pops used to repeat a lot. I think it goes along with the first one. 'A good soldier adapts and overcomes.' You know who said that?"

"That one's gotta be Schwarzkopf."

I shook my head. "Clint Eastwood. It's a paraphrase from *Heartbreak Ridge*."

That made him laugh a little. "I've never seen it."

I raised an eyebrow, Spock-like. "Careful admitting that. You'll get your Man Card revoked."

"Probably deserve it."

"You seen *Tombstone*?"

"Of course."

"*Heat*?"

"Yeah."

"How about *Top Gun*?"

"Sure, but—"

"Your membership card is in no danger. Anyway, the point I'm making is, you did exactly what Clint said. When the plan didn't work exactly as it was supposed to, you adapted and you found a way to overcome." I raised my glass again. "I'd call that a success."

This time, he clinked with some enthusiasm, even spilling a little of his beer down the side of his glass in the process.

We drank.

"Thanks, Bricks."

"Yeah, yeah."

He took another hearty swig of beer, then wiped his mouth. "So now what?"

"Now what? We get paid."

"I know that. I mean, what's next?"

I sipped my beer, thinking. "I guess we do what we've always done. We wait for the next job."

He leaned forward. "Look, I know this one paid pretty good, but for me all that really accomplished was wiping out the expenses I've been running up since our last gig. And that one didn't pay for shit, anyway."

"What's your point?"

"My point is, let's use this one to our advantage. Let it give us some advertising power."

"You want to take out an ad in the *Times*?"

He smiled. "I was thinking more of the *Boston Herald*."

"You're wicked funny."

"Yeah?"

"No. You're an asshole."

He waved me off. "I don't mean the actual paper."

"No shit," I dead-panned. "I thought you were serious."

"I'm saying, let's talk it up around the right circles. Let people know what we've done, and that we're available. I know the people here mostly use their own guys, but there's always situations where someone wants to use an outside contractor like us." His eyes were lit up with excitement. "Hell, the problems they have with Providence alone ought to get us one or two contracts a year. And for the same kind of money we got for this one here, too. Not that nickel and dime crap we get for scaring cheating husbands and smacking around Wall Street types. Hell, we might as well be private eyes if we're going to do that kind of work."

"I don't want to be a PI," I said.

"Neither do I."

"You don't have the mustache for it, Magnum," I told him.

"Neither do you." Then he added, "Yet."

"Fuck yourself."

"Hey, you're part Italian. Give it time."

That was a pretty good one, and I let him have it. Then I thought about his idea for a little while. He waited, pleased with himself. Just for that, I made him wait a little longer before raising my glass to him. "What the hell, Madison Avenue? Knock yourself out."

FIVE
Cameron

In truth, I was in no rush to get back home. The thing with Tia—whatever you could call it—was a bit weird.

She'd been the love of my life back when I was idealistic enough to use phrases like that. Then she made it clear that if I continued with my work and a life with the family, that she'd clock out and we'd be done. I did and she did. She called my bluff.

Then, she came back around and asked me for a favor. She asked me to do the thing she wanted me to stop doing in the first place. She wanted me to kill a guy. A guy who beat her up, and therefore a guy who fucking well deserved it. But still, it was a strange situation.

Cleanest kill of my life, too. No theatrics. No disasters or mistakes. Just did the job and he went away.

So Tia and I kinda got together after that. Almost nine months now, the time it would take to gestate a real life and our little second attempt at love hadn't grown a bit. I think even the strictest anti-abortion nut job wouldn't call it a life yet.

We'd basically stopped sleeping together. I could tell she wasn't feeling it. Each time it felt like she was doing me a favor, like she just wanted it to be over with. I couldn't help feeling like she was trying to jump start her feelings for me again. That she was with me out of obligation for the job I did for her. I wouldn't let her pay me, but she'd found a way to buy me off.

So if I stayed a day or two in Boston, it wouldn't be the end of the world. The whole time I'd been there I kept waiting for her to call and ask when I'd be back. To check in, call to say goodnight or just to hear the sound of my voice. All the things I wanted to do for her. But, no, nothing.

So I sent Bricks home and I extended my hotel room another night.

I called up our contact and told him the job was done, which I assumed he knew already, and told him we'd like to do more business. The commute wasn't too bad, we could work both cities no problem.

He seemed glad to hear the news, said he'd put out the word.

I ate clam chowder on Dartmouth Street. Walked around the Boston Common. Had great Italian on Newbury Street and a drink in a dark bar on Beacon Hill. I was a good tourist for the day. I even went by the marathon finish line to pay my respects, same way I'd done to the World Trade Center after they started letting people in again.

I couldn't tell if it cracked me up or depressed the shit out of me that nobody would be visiting the second stall of the men's room in a certain bar and leaving flowers for a dead man there. Some deaths get holidays, most deaths get forgotten.

I hopped a train back to Grand Central.

Two days later I got the call. A job in Boston again. Our guy had put the word out and someone jumped on it like a lion on a gazelle. I called up Bricks.

"We got another one."

"Yeah?" she said. "I have a meeting tonight too. Things may be looking up."

"Aw, shit, tonight?" I said. "This one is a rush job. He said it's gotta be tonight. I was gonna take the eleven-thirty train."

"I could try to reschedule, but this guy said he could only do tonight. Maybe he was bullshitting me just to fit his own schedule."

I hesitated. I did not want to turn away business, not now.

"Why don't we split this one up?" I said.

"You can handle the Boston job by yourself?"

"You don't sound too sure."

"I'm asking if you're sure. If it's anything like the last one, I don't think you could pick up a guy at a bar."

"Depends on the bar," I said, a smile in my voice. I could tell she was ribbing me, not really concerned I couldn't do a job on my own. After all, we'd met while pursuing our own contracts. "I think I can handle it," I said.

"Okay. I'll take the meeting and hopefully get this one set up down here and between the two it'll be a good month."

"And hey, Bricks," I said. "We still split everything fifty-fifty. I don't want you to think just because I'm doing the Boston job that I'll pocket the money."

"I never doubted it," she said. "But, hey, get a receipt."

I laughed. "Yeah, for tax purposes."

We rang off wishing good luck on both our appointments. I packed a small bag, checked the load in my gun, and headed for the train station.

SIX
Bricks

In the two minutes after Cam hung up, I ran a brush through my hair, unwrapped a stick of gum and popped it in my mouth, slid on my shoes, grabbed my purse, and headed out the door.

I thought about leaving the purse behind, but the fact is that I needed too many things not to bring it. Not just more gum, my keys, a spare tampon, and my wallet, but the short barreled .45 caliber in a strap inside. You never can tell.

The sidewalks were typically crowded, and I wound my way toward the subway. A light queasiness hovered in the pit of my belly. As I walked, I tried to identify the feeling. I decided it was simply excitement. Potentially getting two more contracts on the heels of the German job in Boston felt good. More than good, it was a relief. My bank account had begun to dwindle dangerously close to three figures.

I took the stairs to the subway and caught the first train. I stood near the door, grasping a handle and rocking gently as the train rattled along. The feeling in my gut didn't diminish, and the more I examined it, the less sure I was that it was actually excitement. There was a tug, a nagging worry, at the core of that sense. Yeah, maybe I was excited about whatever Cam had going in Boston, and this evening's prospect, too. But there was something else there.

Or maybe there wasn't. After working the small time cases we'd worked for a while, getting back into what we did best had energized me. I was probably just suffering from the aftermath of all that adrenaline.

I found the restaurant easily enough. It was a small neighborhood place, with just four tables. You saw them around, carving a living out in a city in which restaurants and dining out were closer to religion than recreation. My bet was that most of the places like this fed the same thirty or so people all week long, but what did I know?

This one was Greek, and when I came through the door, it was empty. I glanced at the small clock on the wall to see if I was early, but I was actually five minutes late. So I double-checked the posted hours to see if the place was even open for business. Turned out they'd been open for two hours already.

I was considering leaving when a dark-haired man in a white shirt and a long white apron pushed through the door from the back room. He didn't seem surprised to see me.

"*Despoinída*," he said, dipping his head in slight bow. "Good evening."

"I'm supposed to meet someone," I told him.

"Of course." He gestured toward the tables with his arm. The hair on his forearm was black and thick. "Please."

I walked past him and he led me to the corner table, where he held the chair out for me. I sat. Without hesitation, he bustled away, disappearing into the back. I listened for the sounds of a kitchen restaurant, but outside of the clink of some glass, I didn't hear anything.

The waiter returned with a glass of ice water. "Would you like a cocktail, *despoinída*?"

"Not just yet."

"An appetizer?"

"I'll wait for my friend."

He gave me the slight bow of deference again, and disappeared into the back again.

I sat.

For fifteen minutes.

I sipped my water, and then waited another five.

While I waited, that feeling of unease rattled around inside my gut, but it slowly got burned out with the anger. Pops used to warn me about my temper. He called it *getting my Italian up* and he was convinced there was nothing good that came from it. He may have been right. Once up, my temper burned hot, and then cold. It hung around. The scars I showed Cam courtesy of a pit bull and poor intelligence? That got my temper up, and it stayed up overnight and into the following afternoon when I met with Sal Giordano. That was when the worthless sack of shit was still the boss. I put him on his ass and almost ended up in the East River as a result.

So yeah, temper isn't always a good thing.

Sitting there in the Greek restaurant, waiting for someone I'd never met who was probably going to hire me to kill someone else I'd never met, I tried to tamp down that temper. But goddamnit, the whole thing pissed me off. It was rude. It was unprofessional. You don't set a meet with someone, on your own turf, no less, and then keep them waiting.

You don't—

The front door of the restaurant opened up and two

men walked in. The first was a wiry Italian in a nice suit. He wore an old style Fedora with the brim pulled low. I couldn't figure out if he was trying to be Sam Spade or Frank Sinatra, but I didn't like it either way.

The other man was almost twice the size of the first, and all of it muscle. He entered second, and stopped near the door, crossing his arms like a club bouncer. His head seemed too small for his body, but the rest of his bulk looked proportionate. He radiated raw power even though his expression was flat.

The first man removed his hat and sat down across from me. I recognized him immediately, even though it had been the better part of year since I'd last seen him. He flashed me a smile that looked out of place on his crater-ridden face. The smile didn't touch his eyes.

A cool spike fired from the small of my back out in every direction. I suppressed a shudder.

"The world-famous Bricks," he said, his accent Brooklyn thick. "What a lucky motherfucker I must be to come across you again, huh?"

His name was Abe Fortunato. He'd been a bodyguard for Sal Giordano before the blow-up that brought Cam and me together. I didn't know what happened to him after Sal died, but given that they called him the Italian Ninja, my guess was he landed on his feet.

Behind him, the bodyguard uncrossed his arms, reached out and snicked the door lock into place.

My hand drifted toward the edge of the table. My purse was on the floor to my right. If I went for it, I'd have to be quick.

Fortunato glanced down at my hand, then back into my eyes. That's when his smile turned just a little bit genuine.

Go ahead, those eyes seemed to say. Make it easy.

I stopped moving my hand.

A trace of disappointment flickered his eyes and was gone. His smile broadened but all the sincerity left it.

"Let's talk," he said.

SEVEN
Cameron

The flight to Boston was an easy forty-five minutes, but I wasn't on it. Seems the airlines take a dislike to firearms these days. The train? Bring 'em if you got 'em is their policy.

I had with me a small overnight bag. A change of clothes, a toothbrush, and two .45s plus a .38 as backup. I was carrying more guns than underwear.

I went straight to the meet when I arrived in town. There would be time later to check into the hotel. This new contact wanted to meet ASAP and since the train ride was a few hours longer than by air, I kept my little duffle bag and took the T to the North End—the Italian section of Beantown—looking like I was going to the gym or something.

There's a lot of history in that town, but I couldn't give a shit right then. I was too busy navigating the twisty streets and trying not to notice the smells of pizza coming from every other doorway it seemed. Lunch on the train consisted of a bag of chips that was eighty percent air.

I found the building, a squat little brick deal with a historical marker embedded in the front. They hid out somebody during the Revolutionary War or something. A hideout. Some things never change.

I rang the bell and two burly guys in T-shirts stretched to the limit answered the door.

"You expecting me?" I asked, kinda wishing I'd taken one of the .45s out of my bag before I rang the bell. Bricks is always telling me to plan for the worst and with my record, you'd think I'd always be expecting things to go bad. But these two were waiting for me and they stepped aside and I walked in.

As soon as the door was closed behind me the big guy with a crew cut put a hand on my shoulder.

"Gotta pat you down."

He didn't wait for my permission. I held my duffle in one hand as he slapped at my body like he was beating a rug. I guess I was glad I didn't take my guns out after all. After he'd gone from my collar to my shoes he stepped back and announced, "Clean." I wondered if it was for the benefit of his partner who might have been blind or stupid, or if the lobby was wired and the man who wanted to hire me was watching. This guy, he was cautious. Me, not so much.

Again, they let me go first. On the way up a steep stairway to the second floor every step creaked and the whole place had a slight lean to it. I guess if it's historical enough I should forgive a little tilt after two hundred some-odd years.

Crew Cut leaned in front of me and opened a glass paneled door into an office suite right out of Sam Spade. Dark wood on the floors, big desk, leather chairs, stenciling on the window: FAZZIO & SONS. It didn't say what business father and sons were in together.

A man stood from behind the desk. "You're the guy? Cameron, right?" He was tall and broad shouldered, graying temples added accents to a thick head of hair. He wore a loose gold chain link bracelet and a gold pinky ring with some insignia. Suit jacket over an open collared shirt in black. This guy was class. He was money. He was family in the Italian sense of the word.

"That's me," I said.

He held his arms wide like he was hugging me from across the room, but he made no move out from behind the desk. "Charlie will get your things." Charlie, with the crew cut, took my bag before I could tell him I'd hold on to it.

"Sit, sit," my host said.

The second T-shirted thug set a chair on the rug to face the desk. "Thanks, mister...?"

"Fazzio." He pointed over his shoulder to the window and his name there. He grinned like a politician.

"So," I said. "You got a job needs doing." Small talk is for insurance salesmen.

"I got someone needs to go, yes I do." He twisted his pinky ring, a habit I gathered he didn't even notice any more. "And you come with the bona fides I'm looking for."

"Well, it's nice to make a new connection. I think this could be a long term partnership unless this is a one-off contract." I grinned back at him since I was playing the role of actual salesman now.

"Yeah, you did some pretty high profile work down there in the tri-states."

I know you have to put yourself out there a bit in order to drum up new business, but I didn't like the idea of this guy knowing too much about my past work. Our broker's good word ought to be enough. That's why people in our line use a broker.

"I have experience." I left it at that, but he didn't want

to let it go. I felt a draft come through the room, but the windows were all closed.

"I'll say you do. Heard they call you Slaughterhouse."

This was getting a little chummy for my taste. "Nobody calls me that anymore."

"No, no, you're right," Fazzio said. "Because everybody who did is dead, am I right?"

"I'd prefer to discuss your contract."

"We'll get there," he said. Charlie and his partner flanked the room like the two halves of a vice grip—one on each side of my head.

"If it's better, I can come back later," I said. "I still need to check in to my hotel, get settled. I haven't even taken a piss since I got off the train."

"Ah, shit. Speaking of which," Fazzio said. "Can I offer you a drink?" He pointed to an old style drink cart in the corner. An array of booze bottles, a few warm cans of Coke.

"No, thanks. Let's just talk business and see if we're able to help each other."

"What happened to the long term partnership?"

"I don't even know what this job is and you seem a little reluctant to tell me. Let's take one step at a time."

"Sorry," Fazzio said. He twirled the ring again. I began to wonder if it was some type of signal to the boys behind me. This bastard was making me paranoid. "Kinda like a job interview though, am I right? I need to know who I'm hiring same as you need to know who you're working for."

I exhaled. He was right. The strange vibe I was getting could have been the train ride, the strange city, my full bladder. "I get your point. I think the best thing is for you to let my work speak for me, starting with this job. If I do good work, then we'll work together again."

"Oh, I know you do good work, Cameron." His grin was going and that ring spun like he was going for a record. I should have called Guinness. "Like with Rocco. Now that was a job."

I shifted in my seat, the creak of the leather and the floorboards below me filling the silence. He shouldn't know about that job. It was my final test to make it into the family full time. It also happened to be my uncle. Fazzio knowing about it was bad news.

"You remember that one, right, Cameron?"

"What is this?" I tried to spot my overnight bag in my peripheral vision. It was against the wall and behind Charlie. Not an option.

"Did you know, Cam, that we're related? Yeah, it's true. Third cousins, twice removed or some shit. Distant relations, but, hey—blood is blood, am I right?"

"Is that so?"

"Yeah. Family, Cameron. Nothing more important than family."

I knew then that this was a set-up. My past had crawled into the room and was about to bare its teeth. Very, very sharp teeth that kill.

"I don't know where you're getting your information but—"

Fazzio cut me off with a hand like he was a Supreme telling me to stop in the name of love.

"So if you and me are related, then me and Rocco were related too. Closer than you and me, in fact. Thicker blood."

Man, I really needed that piss now.

"And the thing about family," he said. "You never forget. You never forgive." He stopped twirling his ring long enough to snap his fingers. Charlie and his other half moved like dogs let off a leash. They knew this moment was coming and they'd been ready and waiting. The silent one went behind me and pinned my arms, Charlie came around front and stoically pounded a fist the size and weight of a cannonball into my face.

I toppled back over the chair and fell to the rug. Things had gotten bad and looked to get worse. The only upside for me, not for Fazzio's rug, was that I finally got to piss.

EIGHT
Bricks

"You want some vino?" Fortunato asked me. "It's some Greek shit, but what can you do, am I right?" He motioned at the restaurant around us. "Not like these people know wine."

"No thanks."

"Some ouzo? They got that, of course."

I shook my head, adjusting in my seat to push away from the table just a little bit. My feet drifted to shoulder width apart and I pushed down to feel my footing.

"No? Don't like that licorice taste? Me, neither. How 'bout some caffè, then, huh? It's more like Turkish than anything, but again, whaddaya gonna do?"

I started to say no, but then changed my mind. "Sure. Coffee'd be good. But not the Turkish. Americano."

Fortunato kept his gaze on me while he raised and lowered his hand with two fingers extended. His musclebound bodyguard leaned through the door to the kitchen and spoke in a low voice. I didn't hear anyone answer.

I matched Fortunato's stare. I maintained a neutral expression and forced myself to draw long, deep breaths surreptitiously. I needed to think, and depending on how things went, I'd need the oxygen for more pressing matters than that before long.

Fortunato lit a cigarette. His lighter was a gold plated number with some kind of small gem in the center. As soon as he snapped it shut, I pointed to the cigarette pack. "Can I get one of those?"

He hesitated a moment, then reached for the pack. "I didn't think you smoked."

I didn't answer.

He shook free a cigarette. I took it and leaned forward, the cigarette poised near my lips. "I need a light, too."

He flicked open the lighter and struck the flint in one fluid motion. That was the Fortunato I remembered. All grace and fluidity, if a little overconfident.

I lit the cigarette, using the action to disguise another small slide backwards in my seat. My feet felt solid on the ground. Balanced. To keep him from noticing, I kept my elbows on the table and my eyes on his. "Thanks," I said, my voice flat.

He put away the lighter with a flourish that he pretended he hadn't practiced for hours on end. Being a bodyguard can be long and lonely work while you're waiting outside a door, and anyone with half a brain has to find ways to pass the time. It was pretty obvious what Fortunato did with his.

I blew smoke off to the side. I hadn't smoked in years. Hell, more than a decade. I hoped my lungs didn't betray me. The last thing I needed here was to go to a virgin lung coughing fit.

Fortunato was still watching the cigarette. His insincere smile had faded into something closer to a wry grin. On his acne-scarred face, it didn't look any better than the fake one he'd been sporting before. But truthfully, the only thing that would make him look better was a mask, so what did it matter?

He wagged the two fingers that held his cigarette at me. "You're a naughty girl, Bricks."

"I hear some people pay extra for that."

He let out a short exhalation of smoke in what could have been a laugh. "That's true. People and their ways."

"It takes all kinds."

He took a deep drag and shook his head, then exhaled a long stream of smoke. "Always playing a fucking angle, people, huh?"

"Everyone has an angle."

"'Specially in this city," he agreed.

"What's yours?" I asked.

"Funny you should ask. What do you think?"

I took a shallow puff on the cigarette, then moved it to my left hand. "Is there an ashtray?"

"Use the floor. This place is half a fucking dive. No one will notice."

"A dive? You picked this place."

"Yeah, not for how fancy it was, though."

"Not quite Fucale's, huh?" That was a not-so-veiled barb. Fucale's was a mobbed-up restaurant where Sal used to spend most of his afternoons. That's where he was when I went to see him after the Tommy Davenport pit bull incident. It's where I put the boss on his backside. And Fortunato on his face.

A flash of anger seem to flicker behind his eyes, but it was gone so fast that I wasn't sure I'd seen it. You'd think getting reminded that you got put on your face by a girl would be the kind of memory a bodyguard would get riled about. Fortunato surprised me a little.

"They sold the place," he said. "Fucale's."

"Yeah? The Irish buy it?"

"No. Some Korean family."

The waiter appeared in the kitchen doorway. He swooped in with his small tray holding a regular cup of coffee and a small espresso cup. I got my Americano and Fortunato his Turkish. I didn't take my eyes off of Fortunato, but he glanced up at the waiter and gave him the barest of nods.

When the room was ours again, he lifted his espresso. "What should we drink to? Old friends?"

I picked up my cup. "How about to getting to the point?"

"My kind of toast," he said, and sipped the hot java.

I set mine down without drinking. "Why am I here?"

I already knew the answer, or at least had it narrowed down to two possibilities. He was there to hire me, I hoped. But as an old friend once said, the odds were six to five that he was there to clip me.

Fortunato turned his hands palm up. "You're in business, right? So I'm here to do business."

A third possibility occurred to me. Maybe this motherfucker was wearing a wire.

The collapse and splintering of the Giordano family made some minor news to the public at large, but I'm guessing that it caused earthquake-sized tremors in the law enforcement world. While most cops, local and FBI agents alike, that worked organized crime would be happy to give me a hearty *thank you* for the number I did on Sal, I'm just as sure they'd like to have that conversation while slapping on some silver bracelets.

If they'd manage to pick up Fortunato on some charge and then flip him...

"Who you working for now, Abe?" I asked.

He didn't reply.

"Because I didn't hear," I continued. "I don't know if you went in with Max DaCosta and the boys that came up from Florida, or if you got snapped up by one of the other families. Hell, maybe you started your own crew."

He didn't react.

"Of course, even with your own crew, you'd need someone's blessing to operate, and you'd have to kick some tribute upstairs for that, so it'd be the same as being part of that family. Maybe you'd make more money, but there'd be more risk, too. And you don't strike me as someone who takes a whole lot of risk." I wagged my cigarette at him, miming the gesture he'd used earlier.

"I'm touched you care so much about my livelihood."

"I don't care. I couldn't give half a shit, in fact. But now here we are having coffee, so it makes a girl curious."

He stared at me for a long moment. Then he said, "It don't matter how I make my money, or who with. What matters is that I'm sitting here now."

"Ah. Live in the present. Very Zen."

He shook his head slowly. "Such a wise ass. Last time I saw you, that smart mouth almost got you killed."

"And you saw this from where exactly? The floor?"

That made his nostrils flare slightly.

Good.

"You know, the more I think about it, the more I think you gotta be working for DaCosta. Is he a consigliere for that boss, too? Is he still giving you orders?"

Fortunato's jaw set slightly, then his face relaxed. "Do you want the job I came here to offer you, or not?"

"You mean you're not here to kill me?"

He flicked his cigarette at my face a fraction of a second

before I flicked mine. I aimed for his eyes, and I'd bet he did the same. Both of us missed our targets. His cigarette sailed over my shoulder, dropping a weak trail of sparks in its wake. Mine at least struck him high in the forehead, showering him with ash and embers, and giving me the half second of distraction I was looking for.

"Bitch!" he snarled.

But I was already reaching for the coffee.

NINE
Cameron

I had the sense of being moved, but whether down the street or into the next state I had no idea. When I came to I was in a small room, empty of furniture. The walls were brick and the windows blacked out with newspaper pasted down by glue. The floors were wood and the way they creaked, and the way cracks ran down the bricks in jagged lightning strikes, I figured I was still in Boston, or some similarly old city.

Then I smelled pizza. I knew I hadn't left the North End.

I tried to move, but my hands were tied behind my back. My mouth tasted like blood and I could feel crusted streaks of the dried stuff on my face. I tried to sniff my clogged nose but all I got for the effort was a shooting pain and no air. Probably broken. For sure it was stuffed with clotted blood so I was going to be a mouth breather for a little while.

This Fazzio guy told me we were related, but I'd never heard of him. I didn't doubt it, though. Most Italian family trees were more like vines spreading out in all directions. Big breeders, the Italians.

So they were pissed about Uncle Rocco. Shit.

This was one thing I'd found about killing—one is never enough. You kill one guy, you gotta kill the witnesses. You go in on a set-up and you gotta kill the others who know about it. The only way to come out clean is to strip it down to the finish. Or in my case to pluck every leaf off that family tree.

They'd dumped me on the floor, not even a chair to sit in. The newspaper on the windows was thin enough I could tell it was still daylight out. There was a light fixture in the ceiling with three bulbs, but it was turned off. Still, I could see just fine in the dim room—not that there was anything to see.

I did notice the paper covering the two windows was the *Boston Globe*, so my suspicions were confirmed. I was kind of proud of my little detective work, but I wouldn't let myself be really pleased until I got the hell out of there, and on that front I'd made no headway.

I spun myself on my side and saw the door about ten feet behind me. It didn't look strong, like I could kick it down if I wanted, but even standing up would be hard with my hands the way they were, and as I pulled more I could feel that they had tied my feet too and connected the two ropes so my wrists and ankles were linked together. Yeah, there would be no door kicking for me. No standing up, either.

At least I'd gotten the piss out of the way.

That smell overpowered the distant pizza wafting in from the street. My legs were cold from where the piss had soaked my jeans.

The only good news for me was still being alive. If they didn't have some plan for me I'd be dead already. Of course, the plan could make being hog tied in an empty room seem like a vacation. My people were almost as good at breeding as they were at torture.

I lay and thought about that likely scenario for the next hour.

Finally, the door opened.

I saw three pairs of loafers: one alligator and two polished leather. I turned my eyes up even though I figured it might get me another fist to the face, or maybe one of those fancy shoes.

Fazzio and his two crew cuts.

"He's awake," Fazzio said. His two mutts laughed. "I don't think I've ever seen anybody go down as fast as you did, Cameron." Fazzio smiled down at me. "I mean, I heard of a glass jaw, but you got a glass face."

His audience of two thought he was a riot.

"Untie me and we'll have another round," I said. My words were slurred due to the blood in my nose and on my tongue.

"I bet you want me to bring up your bag," Fazzio said. "Maybe let you lay your hands on that hardware of yours? That more your speed? Huh, Cam?"

"What can I say?" I tried again to snort the plug of dried blood up my nose. No use. "I'm a firm believer in the second amendment."

"I got someone coming by wants to talk to you," Fazzio said.

"Yeah?" I said. "Who's that?" Trying to speak made me figure out I must have bit my tongue when Charlie punched me. One side was swollen and didn't fit my mouth right. Explained the blood in my throat, at least.

"My pop," Fazzio said. "He knew Rocco better than me. He'll want some answers."

So this Fazzio was one of the *and sons.*

"You could have asked first, punched later," I said.

"I had to make sure you'd stick around." He bent down and sat on his heels closer to my face. The Alligator shoes were his. "And that you'd tell the truth."

"I don't lie."

"You better not." He stood, snapped his fingers. A chair scraped across the floor. One of the crew cuts must have brought it in with them. Wooden and old, like everything in this fucking town. Paul Revere probably sat in it before me.

Charlie and his pal lifted me by the arms and untied the link between my hands and feet, then sat me down. Well, threw me down with the chair there to break my fall.

"Then what?" I asked.

"After you talk to Pop?"

I nodded.

"Use your imagination."

Fazzio turned and walked out, his two goons following. I heard the door close and lock, then footsteps on the stairs. A short pause, then another door opened and closed. I was upstairs of the Fazzio & Sons office. I must have been completely out of it if the trip up one flight of steps seemed like a long ride in the country.

I wasn't sure how I could use this information, but I needed as much as I could get if I wanted to get out of there alive. Man, I hoped Bricks' meeting was going better than mine.

TEN
Bricks

A fight can be a surreal experience, even if you've been in your share of them. Things go fast, and there's barely time to think. Yet, at the same time, everything seems to slow down, moving a languid pace that allows you to soak in every little detail, every small nuance.

Intellectually, I know it's all chemical. Hormones get secreted, adrenaline shoots through the body, and it alters our physiology, affecting our perception. But no matter how many times I watch a National Geographic documentary about stress and adrenaline or how many books I read about how martial artists strive to counter those effects, the experience is still a singular mystery to me. How can I move so fast, think so clear, and see everything in slow motion like a John Woo movie? It can't be as simple as chemistry.

Can it?

Those were the odd thoughts flashing through my mind in the time it took me to reach for the cup of hot coffee in front of me, wrap my hand around the cup, and hurl the contents directly into Abe Fortunato's acne-scarred face. By the time the steaming java splashed him, I'd let the question go, tabling it later examination.

If there was a later.

Fortunato let out a high pitched scream and jerked away. His hands flew to his face.

I grabbed the edge of the small table and flipped it

upward, driving the motion from my hips. The force of the blow and the fact he was already leaning backward knocked him over. He crashed to the floor in a heap, the small table on top of him.

The meat at the door was already moving toward me. He bore a neutral, determined expression, as if he were completely unsurprised by this turn of events. Maybe Fortunato got put on his ass all the time, and the bodyguard was used to it. That didn't jibe with Fortunato's nickname, but sometimes people were responsible for making up their own nicknames, instead of earning them.

Either way, I knew I didn't have much time. Fortunato was out for a round or two, but he might recover enough to get involved. And if he had a gun—

Gun!

Of course.

I crouched low and grabbed the strap of my purse. The snaps burst open easily and I reached inside for my pistol.

That's when the meat grabbed me by the shoulders and slammed me backwards into the wall. Darkness flashed across my field of vision, then spots of white. I shook my head to clear it in time to see him cocking his right fist. He held me against the wall, my tip-toes barely touching the floor. I tried to move left, but his grip was vise-like, and I had no leverage. Then the punch was on its way.

Without thinking, I dipped my chin and presented him with the top of my forehead. He didn't have time to react. His fist blasted into my head where the skull is thickest, and he let out a surprised grunt. The force of the blow rattled me, though, and I couldn't take immediate advantage of his surprise. The two of us just held our relative positions, almost as if we were taking a union-mandated break right in the thick of the fight.

He reacted first, while I was shaking off the cobwebs. He gave his hand a loose shake, flexing it twice before making another fist. I didn't want to absorb a second sledgehammer blow, so I snapped my foot straight up into his groin. My kick caught the inside of his thigh and ricocheted into what I thought were his balls, but he only grunted again and narrowed his eyes.

Groin, eyes, throat, they always say. And it has worked for me in the past. So I went for the eyes. He was holding me at an arm's length, crushing my shoulder with his left mitt, but I shot out with my own left hand. I pivoted slightly and extended forward, raking my short fingernails across his eyes.

This time, he didn't scream, but his right hand seemed to forget about punching me and went to his face. In the same moment, I felt the grip on me lessen. I tore free, stepped forward and drove my knee upward between his legs. The top of my knee caught him flush, and I was pretty sure there was no way I missed his jewels this time. The sound he made only reinforced my belief. He let out a gurgling noise that sound like he'd swallowed one of those earlier grunts. Both hands dropped instinctively to cover his groin.

Without hesitation, I raked across his eyes again, getting in a glancing blow. Then I folded my fingers forward and snapped the knuckle-edge of my hand straight into his throat. It wasn't a home run shot, either, but the exhalation of breath and pained expression in his eyes told me it was enough.

I reached into my purse and wrapped my hand around my .45.

Time to get the fuck out of here.

I stepped past the meat, stopping only to deliver a short, downward side-kick to the back of his knee. It wasn't enough to topple him, but he collapsed to the other knee, and that was all I had time for. I bee-lined for the door.

Two steps before I made it, I heard Fortunato cry out. "Bricks! You cunt!"

I stopped.

I shouldn't take things personally. It's a business, after all. All of it. Strictly business, or so they say. And the trademark of a professional is that she can accept that, and deal with it. When people get personal about business, business suffers.

So does personal, come to think of it.

It wasn't even Fortunato's choice of epithet that stopped me. You don't get far in an Italian neighborhood, working around wise guys, without having a C-bomb dropped on you at least once a week. I always believed that *bullets* and *knives* may fuck you up, but *bitches* and *cunts* will never hurt you.

Even trying to clip me, I understood could be business. This line of work had its risks, and one of them was getting blamed for being the instrument someone uses to solve a problem. People seek revenge. All part of that never-ending macho need not to appear weak to one's friends or enemies.

I couldn't complain. That particular group psychosis and cultural dysfunction was why I had a career in the first place. But now it had resulted in someone deciding it was a smart business move to hit the hitter.

The question was, why?

And more importantly, who?

I turned back to Fortunato. He'd pulled his hands away from his face and was pawing at his ankle for whatever small caliber piece he kept there. I kicked him in the side, and he let out another scream. Then I dropped my weight onto his chest, resting my knee on him.

"You scream like a third grade girl, Abe," I told him.

"Fuck you, you fucking dyke cunt fucking—"

I pressed the barrel of my .45 to his forehead. He gave a start and another abbreviated cry of pain as the metal touched his scalded skin. Then he slowly raised one of his hands. He kept the other hand covering one eye that got the worst of the coffee. I wondered for a moment if he'd lose the eye, or have to wear a patch.

"Who sent you?" I asked him.

He shook his head.

I pressed harder. "Who?"

He didn't reply. I glanced over at the meat and saw him coughing and rubbing his face. I didn't have long before he'd recover enough to come at me again. Even though he was roughly the size of a rhino, I knew I could stop him with the .45 if it came to it. But I didn't want to kill him if I didn't have to. Sure, he'd just attacked me but the reality was, he was just being a loyal soldier. He didn't choose the mission.

Fortunato did, though. I had no doubt about it. And I probably had all of about four seconds to convince him to tell me who gave him that mission before my advantage evaporated and I was dealing with the meat again, or some cook appeared from the kitchen, or a beat cop came through the door.

Unfortunately, I didn't have any stellar interrogation ideas on such short notice, so I settled with a third push of my gun into his forehead. "I'll shoot you in the face, Abe. I swear I fucking will, and it'll be a goddamn improvement. Now tell me who sent you here? Was it DaCosta?"

He looked at me out of his one good eye with pure hatred and disgust. Where his hand wasn't covering, his cratered face was heavily splotched with red. I knew he wasn't going to answer me. He was old school, and I had to respect that, if a little grudgingly.

I started to turn away to leave before the meat came back online, but then I saw Fortunato's mouth twitch so I hesitated. Maybe I was wrong. Maybe he wasn't as hardcore as I thought. Maybe he was going to talk.

"Who sent you?" I prompted him again. "Tell me."

"I'll tell you," he growled back. His lips pulled back in an insane, leering smile. Then he said, "It was your nigger-lovin' mother, you bitch!"

He spit up at me but I barely noticed. I stood, leveled the gun at his forehead and squeezed the trigger. The sudden barking of the muzzle filled the room. His blood splattered on the floor beneath and beside him. The crazy, hateful expression in his eyes faded into a blank stare.

I shot him twice more, both times in the face.

Then I changed my mind about the meat, and emptied the rest of my magazine into his back before I left the café.

Because this wasn't business.

It was definitely personal.

ELEVEN
Cameron

Hunger and thirst. The need to wash up, especially my piss-soaked jeans. I'd have killed even for a TV to watch or something better to look at than the drab walls and newspaper covered windows.

After Fazzio left they hadn't turned on the light and the sun moved off toward California so the room grew ever murkier. I'd tried to loosen my hands and felt like I was getting a little somewhere. Maybe if they left me locked in here for another two weeks I'd squeeze my way out. But when I heard footsteps on the stairs outside I knew my appointment had arrived. Fazzio Sr. had come to survey the boy's work.

My back was to the door so when it opened I heard voices, but couldn't see who they belonged to. I recognized the younger Fazzio at least.

"Wait, who?"

"Fortunato," said a gruffer, deeper voice.

"In the face?"

"More than once."

My neck was turned as far as it would go. Finally Fazzio stepped into view and brought the old man with him. Senior had the protruding gut of a man who liked his pasta and hated exerting himself. His suit was expensive, but who did he think he was impressing? He wore gold accents from everywhere they would hang. Some of these old school types wore more jewelry than a call girl.

Fazzio Sr. didn't introduce himself. He started right in, "Lemme tell you a story."

He planted his feet shoulder width apart in front of me, crossed his hands in front of his crotch.

"Rocco and I worked together a little bit in the eighties. Must seem like ancient history to a kid like you. Last fucking century. He was up here and we were taking a break, seeing the sights in the combat zone. That night I had the best pussy of my entire life." He turned to his son. "And that includes your mother." Fazzio Sr. crossed himself. "God rest her soul."

He turned back in my direction, though he was talking to the air.

"Me and Rocco hit a strip club specialized in Asian chicks. Chinese, Japanese, I don't know what the fuck they were. We'd done some work that day making way for a new pipeline of merchandise to come through from Thailand so we were in a rice eating mood, y'know? He gets a dance, I get a dance. The chick I had was okay. No tits, crooked teeth. Nothing to write home about." He smiled, nodded his head at the memory. "Chick he had, though, was so damn hot. Tiny little thing. Teenager, but knew how to move her body, y'know? So you know what he does? Rocco? He says to me, he says, 'You take her.' Just gives her up to me. Says I look like I could use it more. And, man, that girl could fuck the entire Chinese army and still be tight as virgin. In fact, now that I remember it, she kept playing Madonna on the tape deck. That 'Like A Virgin' song, over and over." His eyes went distant into some reverie. "Best pussy I ever had."

He took a step toward me and leveled his gaze directly at my eyes for the first time. "That's the kind of guy Rocco was." His voice dropped low, "And you popped him."

What could I say? I couldn't deny it.

"You think I liked doing it?"

"Did I ask what you like or dislike?"

"He brought me in. Gave me a job. He was my uncle, for fuck's sake."

"So why'd you do him?"

"Because it was my job."

Fazzio Sr. traded a look with Junior as he stood straight. "And that's why I'm here. And why you're here. Who gave the order?"

It made sense why they kept me alive. They knew I was only the trigger man. A low level like me would never make the call to take out Rocco, so it had to come from somewhere. Sadly though, he was about to be disappointed.

"I already beat you to it," I said.

Father and son gave me the same cocked eyebrow look.

"I already killed the man who gave the order."

"You got a name?"

"Sal."

They exchanged looks again. They knew Sal was dead. They had to know it was only Sal who could give an order like that.

"Looks like this was just a big waste of time, gentlemen," I said. If there was an apology coming from them, they hid it well.

"So it was you behind the whole thing with Sal and all that shit?"

"Yeah." I didn't know whether to be proud or not.

"Nobody else?"

"What do you mean?"

"Where's Bricks?"

How did she get into this? Shit. They wanted us both.

"She had nothing to do with Rocco."

"I heard you two were working together."

"Only after. Well, starting with Sal."

Shit. I was spilling a whole lot of beans here. Behind my back I started working on the ropes again.

"So where is she now?"

"I don't know. Not here. Not in Boston."

"I know that."

"Then you know as much as me."

Fazzio Sr. clapped his hands in front of him, angry and looking for something to smack.

"Fucking waste of time," he growled.

"I agree," I said. "Let's cut our losses and call it a day, huh? Maybe let's say I stay the hell away from Boston, okay? You won't ever see me again."

Senior turned on me, his eyes red hot with rage. "Rocco was your own fucking blood."

Fazzio Sr. reached down and grabbed my shirt. I was powerless to do anything. He lifted and I rose up, the chair with me. The old man was still strong. His wide chest hadn't lost its power, even if his waistline had lost the battle long ago.

With a grunt and a grizzly bear growl, he spun me and charged at the window. I swiveled my head around, wondering if I was going through or not. My back hit, the chair cracking against the pasted-over glass and shattering it. My head banged on the window frame where the two halves of the windows met. The bottom half was a mess of glass shards and broken wood. The latch held and the top half still bore *Boston Globe* headlines from three years ago.

The old man shoved me forward until my upper torso went out the window, leaning back on the chair still tied to me. Junior and the muscle didn't move to stop the old man from his threat to drop me three stories down. The old man's face was too close to mine.

"You don't do that to blood."

I didn't know if it would help reminding him that we were related too, however distant. I figured my sins had cut those ties already. The rules were hard to follow and kept changing.

My feet were up off the floor. He shoved harder and I leaned farther out. My arms behind my back slid along the broken edge of the window. A shard of glass cut along my arm taking a deep slice from where my biceps started, arcing across and down below my elbow. I let go with a howl of pain.

He thrilled in my agony. "That's it, punk."

Sweat beaded on his forehead as he soaked through his thousand dollar suit. He'd put all his strength into lifting me and now he seemed spent. He puffed for air, but seemed to delight and even draw strength from my pain.

I felt blood flow down my arm, soak into the back of my jeans.

I felt something else.

The jagged edge of the window hadn't broken cleanly, probably due to the layers of glue and newspaper stuck there. Like vicious teeth the edge of the glass cut at me, but also at the ropes. My arms, now slick with blood, moved under the ropes, and the ropes sagged loose, frayed from the cuts of glass.

"Rocco was a fucking saint," he spat at me. Maybe a little overboard, but everyone looks better in death. I only hoped I wouldn't find out how I looked in the next few seconds.

I heard Junior say, "Pop."

"A fucking saint!"

"Pop! Not like this. Not here."

Junior put a hand on his dad's arm. I knew full well this was how it's done. You get someone else to do the dirty work. The big man didn't wrinkle his suit.

My head faced up to the darkening sky overhead. I could hear street sounds below, smell the tomato sauce. My arm hurt like a son of a bitch and I bled like crazy.

Junior begged his dad again for restraint. Fazzio Sr. relented and tugged me back inside. My head knocked against the window frame again and the jagged teeth of the glass bit at the ropes. They went slack on my wrists.

My spine sent a sharp spike of pain through me when the chair slammed to the floor. Senior stepped back, weaved like a drunk, and panted for breath.

"Charlie will take care of it," Fazzio Jr. said. "We don't need a body on the street, okay, Pop?"

I swear I could hear the dripping of my own blood as my arm emptied out onto the floor.

"Yeah," Senior said. "Take care of this fuck. Then take care of his cunt girlfriend." He turned to Junior. "Find her. Fucking find her."

I'm not sure how Bricks would take to being called a cunt. Something told me—not well.

Things had gotten chaotic enough, and the rate I was bleeding out threatened to do the job before Charlie had a chance, I need to make a move. Any move.

"What happened to the girl?" I said.

An awkward stillness came over the room. Senior's wheezing breath was the only sound.

"The dancer. What happened to her if she was such a good lay?"

Senior looked at his son like, *You believe this fucking guy?*

"She got deported. How the fuck should I know?"

"I just thought maybe you'd want to keep seeing her, seeing as she was so good." Time to go for broke. "And obviously because your dead wife was a dried up cunt."

Fazzio Sr. charged. I slid the hand from my uninjured arm out from the tangle of loose ropes with a shard of glass gripped tightly in my fist. I felt it close to cutting into my palm, but I had to hold on. The arc of my swing met Fazzio's sweaty face as he neared me. The glass carved deep into his cheek. I saw the whites of his molars through the open gash before he screamed and fell to the floor clutching his face.

I stood. Fast. I swung the shard of glass around to my left and caught Junior in the shoulder. The glass bit into my hand and I let it go, but I'd gotten him decently so he leaned back away from me, not anxious to get bloodied. Not while he had muscle in the room with us.

Charlie was torn between helping the old man and attacking me. His hesitation was all I needed to grab the chair and swing it. The sturdy legs banged across the thick arm he raised to block. I let it bounce off him and reversed my swing. The rebound shot caught him in the temple.

The big man tilted and went down. I dropped the chair as my arm with the long slice in it buckled and couldn't hold the weight any longer. But all three men were down for the moment at least. I saw the open window and the open door. I'm not fucking Spiderman. I turned for the door and ran.

TWELVE
Bricks

I couldn't go home.

I'd moved from my old apartment after the whole Sal debacle. Finding a new place in this city was a bitch, but I managed to ferret one out that met my needs. It felt more like a hotel room than a home, but that was okay, too. Maybe I was in transition.

Only now it probably wasn't safe. If someone had gone to the trouble of setting me up with a fake job interview, maybe they'd done enough research to find where I lived. And now that the cat was out of the bag as to their foiled plans, the next move would be to send the infantry to my apartment and finish the job.

So I found a bookstore in a neighborhood I'd never spent any time in before. They sold coffee at the front and had stacks and stacks all the way to the back wall, interspersed with small tables in odd places. I didn't want any coffee, but I bought some anyway. I pulled a random book off a shelf and took a tiny, rickety table in a corner behind one of the shelves. I tried calling Cam to tell him what happened but it went to voice mail. I told him to call me as soon as he got my message and hung up. Then I flipped open the book, stared down at it, sipped my coffee, and commenced to try to figure out what the mercy fuck was going on.

Forming a logical chain of thoughts was difficult, because a steady anger pulsed in my chest. A rash of different kinds of emotions fueled that anger. I tried to sort through the contempt, the sense of outrage, and betrayal.

Without a doubt, Fortunato was going for the jugular when he spat out his last curse at me. That's how all old school Italians think. Everything is always about family, whether it's love or duty or curses.

The funny thing is, my pops served the family well. He could certainly act as a button man, and I think that was how he actually saw himself, though in reality, he was more of a utility player. When they needed someone to make a delivery, he could handle it. If someone needed a reminder when it came to paying back the loan in a timely manner or showing the proper respect, he could handle that too. If you needed someone who could ride shotgun on a truck hijacking, or add some muscle to a card room, you could always call Brickey. And if you've got the boss's son driving up a hijacked truckload of untaxed cigarettes from out of state, who do you think they decided to send along to Obi-Wan the youngster on the trip?

Pops.

Ironically, it was that last role that got him arrested and sent to prison for what ended up being the rest of his life. Dumbass Sal brought along his favorite gun, a chrome plated .357 caliber, instead of a throwaway. So instead of tossing the gun as soon as they were clear and on the road, he kept it on him after they cleared the hijacking. Too valuable to give up, I guess.

When the state troopers converged on them still fifteen miles out of state, Sal panicked. But Pops took care of things. He took the gun, and he took the rap, and Sal ended up pleading out to a minor beef as an accomplice while Pops went to the joint. And it was there that he got sick, and there that he died, and all the while, he didn't say word one to anyone about anything. He was old school, and I understood him to the bone.

Damn straight.

My mother, I wasn't quite as clear on.

I never really quite understood what brought the two of them together, for one thing. I couldn't remember any domestic strife any more than I could remember domestic bliss. Instead, their relationship seemed...workman-like. She was the Italian Mafia princess, or a duchess at least, and them being together is probably what gave a mutt like him an entrée into the family. Of course, once in the door, he earned his own keep and rose on his own merit. But she had been his golden ticket.

So maybe they were only doing what they both needed to do. She was supposed to marry someone from the neighborhood. Preferably an Italian, but definitely someone in the life. He wanted to be more than a small timer that kicked up to the family. So I guess they both got their wish.

Only I don't think *wish* is the right word where my mother is concerned. I think *duty* fits the bill better. She did her duty, and I never heard her complain. But when Pops went away to prison, it didn't take long for her to take up with a doctor at the neighborhood clinic. Theirs was a secret, passionate affair, and a dangerous one. If anyone from the neighborhood found out, and told someone in the family, the kind doctor would get a visit that would be very unlike the ones he was used to.

For more than one reason. Messing around with another man's wife brought a price with it in that neighborhood. It still did today. But a black man messing with a white man's wife? Christ, it was like it was still 1952 or so where that was concerned.

That was probably why she ran off with the guy. It was really the only way they could be together. And jetting off to parts unknown into some kind of self-imposed witness relocation program was also the only way she could keep her lover safe.

Her lover. The words still sound strange to my ear. Though he's probably her husband now, in spirit if not in law. And you know what I say?

Salud, Ma. Be happy. It's not like there's much happiness in this world anyway, so you gotta grab onto it when you have the chance. Maybe you could've let your daughter know you're still alive out there somewhere once in a while, but still...salud. I can forgive the silence. I get it.

And yeah, truth be told, maybe I've still got a few anger issues there. But that's between Ma and me. It's not for some piece of dog shit like Abe fucking Fortunato to talk about, or throw in my face. He doesn't have the right, and neither does whoever sent him.

I actually once met the doctor she ran off with. He fixed me up when I broke a finger. My take, he was a nice man, with an easy way about him, one that settled a person down. I could see how he was good at his job, and I could see how my mother would be attracted to him. And since Pops was in prison with what might as well have been a death sentence, it wasn't like the good doctor was stealing away his bride, either.

Of course, that's not how my family saw it, especially the Italian side. No, my mother was a traitor to them. A traitor for leaving Pops and the family, and a traitor for having the audacity to see the doctor for something more than the color of his skin. I spent way too many Sunday dinners over the years listening to discussions on the topic, until I put an end to it by not going to Sunday dinners most of the time. Of course, in Italian families, the not talking about something can be just as loud.

So when Fortunato called Ma a "nigger-lover," he thought I would feel the same way about her choice and the good doctor that he and most of the family did. And he was hoping that those feelings and his words would make me angry.

He was right about the last part. They did. The whole thing pissed me off right down to my core. But not because of who my mother fell in love with. Or even that she ran off, though that still has some sting. No, what got me the most was the self-righteous condemnation of people like Fortunato. How they saw my mother and the doctor. How they looked down their noses at the both of them like they were somehow so much better...all of them liars, thieves, pimps, and killers.

But which one of them sent Fortunato?

I pressed the heels of my palms to my eyes and rubbed. The weariness of a post-adrenaline crash swept over me, coupled with the heaviness of the emotion I was feeling. When I opened my eyes again, I saw that my coffee was barely touched. I brought it to my lips. Cold. I drank it anyway, letting the caffeine do its thing. I needed to think, not walk down memory lane or wallow in pissed off sentiments.

The taste of Fortunato's cigarette was still on my tongue, despite the coffee and the passage of time. I didn't want another one, but I longed for the distraction. Something to help me break from the feeling in my chest, and the memories that this had evoked.

DaCosta, I thought, and took a deep breath.

It had to be DaCosta.

Max DaCosta was Sal's consigliere, right up to the end. According to Sal, right before I shot the worthless piece of shit, DaCosta had jumped ship and joined the Florida crew that was muscling in on Sal's territory at the time. It was a smart move, a real Tessio play, only in DaCosta's case, it worked out.

If Sal told the truth, and DaCosta worked for the Florida crew now, it only followed that he'd pick up a guy like Fortunato, and bring him along. They had history, and it gave DaCosta someone in his new family that he could trust. It's what I would have done. I couldn't be sure from Fortunato's reaction at the Greek diner if that was how it went, but I couldn't rule it out, either.

So say Fortunato was working for DaCosta, and DaCosta was working for the Florida crew. I knew next to nothing about those guys. The boss was some younger buck name Trepani. Carlo, I was pretty sure. Trepani laid claim to the territory Sal controlled through his grandfather. Sal's father sent Carlo's gramps to Florida back in the sixties for some reason, but I didn't know what it was. Maybe to watch over family interests there, or set up a satellite operation. Hell, maybe they simply flat out exiled the guy. In any event, Carlo Trepani decided it was time to come home, and he pushed Sal pretty hard.

Cam told me something else, too. That his Uncle Rocco was going over to Trepani, and had tried to woo Cam to go with him. And if Rocco was planning on going, I'd guess a few others were as well. Sal probably would've lost the war even if Cam and I hadn't intervened.

So you'd think Trepani and his consigliere would be thrilled with us. We cut the head off the snake, and made their job of taking over that much easier. Why try to kill me now?

Me.

"Hunh," I grunted, the sound barely audible.

What if it wasn't just me? What if it was us? If so, they'd be laying for Cam when he got back from Boston. Or maybe that Boston meet was a setup, just like mine.

I thought about it for a little while, but I couldn't be sure. I tried Cam's number again, and got no answer again. But that didn't mean anything. Hell, he could be asleep. His battery could have died. Maybe he was getting laid by some Southie girl.

I hoped for any of the three.

But even if they were after us both, the question was still why?

Did they think we knew something? Or was it some guinea honor bullshit about how it wasn't our place to take out Sal? That our actions prevented Carlo from fulfilling his destiny of vengeance? Or that, even though they were happy with what we did, we still killed a boss and how dare we?

It seemed a little far-fetched to me.

But only a little.

My head hurt. I realized I'd been clenching my jaw hard enough to cause the headache. Forcing my muscles to relax, I breathed slowly and deeply. I stopped thinking about everything, or at least tried to. Fortunato's sneer kept popping into my mind's eye, and his last words echoed in my head. But little by little, I pushed even that aside, and for a few moments at a time, at least, I achieved some measure of stillness.

The sudden hand on my shoulder interrupted all of that.

They'd found me.

I knew instinctively that I didn't have time to stand. I'd be lucky if I had a full second before the next move came, which I fully expected was a knife to the chest or across the throat. I reacted without thinking, reaching toward the hand at my shoulder with both hands. My thumbs and fingers found their grip, and I rotated all of my upper body toward my center, twisting my attacker's hand, executing sankyo. The move turned his hand outward, palm up, then backward at the wrist. I drove the hold downward, forcing him to his knees in front of me. I used the momentum to stand, then transitioned to an arm bar. I had already started to hyper-extend the elbow when his voice stopped me.

"Stop, please!" he screamed, already in tears. "I'm sorry, I'm sorry, I'm sorry."

It took me a second to recognize him. He didn't have the look of someone DaCosta would send. His long scraggly hair was pulled back in a ponytail. His round glasses were askew on his face, which bore look of pain and surprise. Then I realized he was the guy I'd bought my coffee from at the front of the store.

Shit. He worked there, and had only been checking on me. I loosened my grip, then helped him to his feet. "It's all right," I said. "I didn't mean—"

He pulled away from me with another cry, turned around, and ran, flailing his arms and knocking over books along the way. "Help!" he yelled. "Somebody help me!"

So much for remaining incognito.

I grabbed my purse and got the hell out of there.

THIRTEEN
Cameron

I hit the streets leaving a trail of blood Stevie Wonder could follow.

I hung a right once I hit the sidewalk, ran between two old brick-sided buildings, took two lefts, turned into an alley between buildings, and ducked into a parking garage. I had no clue where I was. The streets weren't in a New York grid and I'd run in circles for all I knew. I tucked myself into the gap between a chain link cage for garbage cans and an elevator.

I peeled my hand away from my sliced arm. The blood had started to dry and grip my palm in place. It came off to reveal a hand print which quickly got pasted over by a fresh flow of blood. The whole thing throbbed a dull, all-over pain. The tender bruises and crooked nose from Charlie's fist didn't even register on the pain scale anymore.

A car came down the ramp toward the exit. I huddled in my notch like a rat as the headlights swept over me. The car's tires squeaked over the painted arrows showing the way out. I wish my direction was that clearly marked.

I knew I couldn't stay, but I had nowhere to go. My guns, along with my change of clothes, my wallet and my phone were all upstairs at Fazzio & Sons. I didn't chance going back there, even if they were all out on the street looking for me, which I had to assume they were.

A hospital would ask questions about my cut. At least it

wasn't a gunshot they'd have to report to the police, but with no ID it would be hard to get attention from an ER. And if Fazzio was smart, a hospital is the first place he'd check.

More Italian food smells wafted through the air, but I was no longer hungry. Not with the marinara I was leaking from my arm all over the Freedom Trail. Everywhere I turned in the North End little markers told me the historical significance of the ground on which I stood. Pretty soon it would only be significant to me as the place where I bled out.

Like my rat brethren I poked my head out skittishly, nose twitching for signs of danger. Nobody on the street. I ventured out, grateful to be away from the smell of garbage.

An occasional car passed by, but they paid me no mind. The streets were mostly residential, short and old looking. I crossed over Hanover Street—too busy, made me nervous. I went deeper into the smaller side streets. Went past a church and thought about asking for asylum there, but there would be questions and plus, churches made me nervous too.

One sign did seem promising. I didn't know what I was searching for but any port in a storm, right?

The tailor shop door rang an electronic bell as I stepped over the threshold. I expected a little brass number, but times change. From the look of the old school shop, it was about the only nod to modernity they'd made.

The lighting was slightly yellow from fixtures colored by time and nicotine. Behind the small counter was an elaborate series of piles—suit jackets, women's pants, dress shirts. It looked wonderfully disorganized in a way only the proprietor would know what the hell was going on.

"Hello?" My voice sounded more mouse than rat.

"We're closed," came a woman's voice from the back. "Vincent!"

There was rustling from behind a faded red curtain separating the back room from the customer portion of the store.

"You forgot to turn the sign around again," the woman scolded.

A man came backing through the part in the curtain. Vincent, I assumed. He wore a white tank top with white chest hair sprouting from the neck line above where he had a linen napkin tucked, covered in fingerprints of red sauce. His jaw worked a mouthful of food and he lifted the napkin, dabbed at his mouth while he waved a placating hand to the voice behind him.

He swallowed, tucked the napkin in his back pocket and smiled at me. His face scrunched up into a bouquet of wrinkles.

"How can I help you?"

"I don't mean to intrude."

He waved a dismissive hand back at the curtain. "Don't mind her. She'd like me to keep bankers hours, but that don't pay the bills."

His voice was thick with Boston, his eyes kind and his shoulders stooped with the years of his trade. He saw my arm.

"What's that there?" A wariness crept into his voice.

"I didn't know where else to go..." I hated sounding so desperate.

"You in trouble?"

"None that I'm bringing with me," I said, hoping to allay his fear. "Just got in a bit of a scrape is all."

"Not from around here," he noticed.

"No. And I didn't exactly get a warm welcome."

"Southern hospitality we ain't got around here." He stepped closer to me, picked up a pair of half glasses off the counter from a mess of things I hadn't even noticed. He peered at my cut.

"Nasty," he said.

I looked down, worried I was dripping on his floor, but the flow of blood seemed to have stopped for the moment.

"Hurts like a son of a bitch, too," I said.

I felt like this guy was my people. Old school Italian. Believed in his work. He'd obviously been in business a good long while. That meant customers trusted him. It meant he knew the neighborhood he worked in and probably little would surprise him.

"Vincent, your pasta's gettin' cold," the woman's voice called.

"Sorry to interrupt your dinner," I said.

"Another plate of linguini. Nothing new. Now this..." He moved closer and examined my arm. "This is new."

"I take it you're good with a needle and thread?"

He turned his eyes from my arm to my eyes, peering over the top of his glasses. His breath smelled like garlic and tomatoes, the wrinkles in his face like a map of Sicily.

"Been a while since I sewed anything but fabric."

"But you've done it?"

"Before you were born, most likely. Do I wanna know who did this to you?"

"I doubt it."

"Try me on for size," the tailor said.

I hesitated. Could be I'd walked in on a close family friend of either Fazzio or Sons. Oh well, my arm wasn't gonna stitch up itself.

"Guy named Fazzio."

Vincent turned away from me, said, "Gah," like he'd gotten a bad clam in his linguini. "That son of a whore been causin' trouble in this neighborhood since before I got my dick wet." He turned and spat ceremoniously on the floor. "I hope you got him back twice has good."

"Maybe half as good," I said.

This made the old man happy. "No shit? You gave him what for?"

"Did my best."

Vincent chuckled to himself, took off his glasses and cleaned them on his shirt. Without looking at me he said, "You family?"

"Not any family around here."

"New York by that silly accent," he said. He was one to talk.

"Things have been complicated, but I earned my keep."

Vincent inhaled deeply like he was trying to smell a memory.

"Those were the days," he said. "Cadillacs on the curb and minks on the women. You settled a score like men and lived by a code."

Jesus, I'd stepped right into Don Corleone's tailor shop. Vincent would have loved talking to Uncle Rocco.

"So before I bleed all over your floor, you gonna help me out or what?"

Vincent turned and began to rummage around behind the counter. "Wouldn't be the first time," he said. "Come around here."

I moved behind the counter where only a narrow walkway seemed carved out of the piles of clothes and the glass front countertop, the inside displays of buttons, cuff and collar options way out of date and ignored now behind smeared and pock-marked glass.

"Vincent, your dinner." His wife came through the curtain. She stopped when she saw me behind the counter. She was squat and round. Thick ankles and dull gray hair in a tight bun. "Who the hell is this? We're closed."

"Speaking of," Vincent said, not looking up from his sewing kit open before him, "lock the door, Loretta."

"Some people got no respect for posted business hours," she said.

"The door, Loretta."

"Why should I?" She crossed her arms in defiance. She hadn't noticed my wound and even if she had I don't think she would have given a shit if it meant her pasta got any colder.

"Because if you don't I'm not gonna give you a poke tonight when I come to bed."

This made her frustrated, but she did march to the front of the store and locked the door, then turned the OPEN sign around to CLOSED. She passed by us and through the curtain without another word.

"Forty-six years," Vincent said. "Never gets dull."

He turned around holding a heavy needle threaded with black string.

"This is gonna suck," I said.

"That drawer there," he said, pointing. "Some whiskey."

I opened the drawer and lifted out a fifth, half gone. I unscrewed the cap and was about to lift it to my lips when

Vincent stopped me with a school teacher-like, "Ah-ah." I brought the bottle down and handed it over.

"This first," he said and then without warning doused my arm with the liquor. Fuck me, it hurt more than the original cut from the glass. I bit down so hard I thought my teeth would crack. He handed me back the bottle, now three quarters gone.

"You done good," he said, "to keep from screaming."

"I figured Loretta would frown on that." I took my first drink.

"That she would, that she would." He fitted his glasses on the end of his nose. "Shall we?"

I tilted the bottle and drank until it was empty. Not nearly enough.

"We're not even gonna wait until that sinks in a bit?"

"Pain now or pain later. Either way, don't get pissed at me, get pissed at Fazzio."

"Oh, I'm already pissed at them."

"You and half this city."

Vincent adjusted my arm so the cut faced him. He didn't flinch at the open flaps of skin. To him they must have been nothing more than panels of cotton blend.

"Hey, thanks," I said. "You're really helping me out here."

"No, thank you," he said. "I haven't had this much fun in years."

And with that he drove the needle into my arm.

FOURTEEN
Bricks

I took the subway to the Village and got a sandwich and some ice water at a small diner, but I couldn't relax. Maybe it was because the diner had an eerie, hole-in-the-wall resemblance to the one Fortunato tried to ambush me in. But more likely, it was that feeling of being hunted that I couldn't shake.

And I didn't like it one bit.

I'd spent my entire adult life being the hunter. It wasn't like Sal sent me a contract on a weekly or even monthly basis, but it was frequent enough that it seemed like I was always on a job or preparing for one. When you're a button man, you're a predator looking for prey. Being treated like prey didn't sit well with me.

In sports, business, and war, they say the best defense is a vigorous offense. That philosophy wasn't very much in keeping with what I'd learned in the aikido dojo, but it fit my world experience. So I decided it was time to turn the tables.

I still couldn't be sure who was behind the attempted hit, but that only meant I'd have to play the odds. And the best odds were on the Florida crew. I didn't know exactly why Trepani would want me dead, but this business didn't run on logic much of the time. There were a lot of testosterone-fueled decisions that got made, and even the bosses in this business were more like Tony Soprano than Vito

Corleone when it came to keeping their heads. Logic did not always rule the day.

My bank was a national chain, and I found one just a few blocks from the diner. They had an ATM outside. The balance in my checking account was pretty paltry, and the savings wasn't looking a whole lot better. Still, there was enough to run on, if I decided that was the best course. I mean, at least as far as Cleveland.

My response to that idea was immediate. No way. As far as I was concerned, the world barely existed outside the five boroughs. This was my home, and I wasn't going to be pushed out by some mouth breather.

That's your pride talking.

I withdrew some cash, stuffed it in my pocket, and walked down the crowded sidewalk, considering that thought. No question, it was true. But I was old enough to know that just living wasn't enough in this world. You had to live your life, your way. If you didn't do that, you weren't living. You were existing.

Sal tried to run me out, or kill me. He failed. I wasn't going to let Trepani do that to me, either.

The rational side of my brain kicked in, reminding me that while I'd defeated Sal, there had been a particular set of circumstances aiding me. For one, his empire was under siege at the time from these very same Florida boys. Secondly, I had a lot of inside information on Sal's operation, since I'd been part of it for years. And thirdly, I had some considerable help near the end from Cam.

Cam.

Damn it.

I stepped up against a building and pulled out my cell phone, checking for missed calls. None. Just for the hell of it, I called him again. It went straight through to voicemail. That meant his phone was turned off. Or that the battery died. Or that it was with him at the bottom of the Charles River.

I forced those negative thoughts out of my head. Cam was a survivor. His work might seem sloppy, but it really wasn't. The results sometimes were, but in the end, he got the job done. And if something was going on in Boston, he'd handle it. I couldn't spend my time worrying about him if I was going to get my job done.

Of course, if I found out his phone was still off so he could enjoy some down time with some Barbie doll from Southie, I'd kick his ass.

That made me smile, mostly because if I'd said it to him, I knew it'd make him smile, too.

I pushed away from the wall and walked probably a mile as leisurely as I could. There's a rhythm to walking these streets, and you somewhat had to go with the flow, unless you wanted to be like the slow car in the passing lane. This wasn't Trepani's territory, so I wasn't as worried about standing out, but blending in was still the smart policy. So call it a brisk stroll.

The problem I faced was that Trepani's crew was all new to me. I didn't know their names or their faces, with the exception of Max DaCosta, the consigliere. And Fortunato, of course. But human nature resisted change. People wanted to know where to go to place a bet, to borrow a buck, or to ask a favor. The men in this business knew human nature. So when a new boss like Trepani moved in, did it make sense for him to change up all the storefronts? Or was the better course to simply co-opt these existing locales, places that people already knew to go?

That made sense to me.

I kept walking, and thinking, and somewhere along the way, I figured out what my next move would be.

Albertini's barber shop held some bittersweet memories for me. I didn't want to go there, but it seemed like the safest place to start. On the face of it, the shop appeared to be nothing more than a four-chair establishment filled mostly with old-time barbers. But if someone looked a little closer, they'd notice that not everyone who came through the door stayed long enough to sit in one of those chairs. That's because Albertini's had been an active front for the family's betting for years.

They used to have a single man handling the bets. Arthur Zucarello. Zooker, they called him. Memories of him brought a painful lump to my throat, but I swallowed hard and pushed it down. When it didn't go away, I took a deep breath and thought about Zen and living in the present moment. The irony of when I chose to embrace sensei's philosophies and when I rejected them wasn't lost on me, but damned if that lump didn't go away.

Mostly.

I didn't know who took over for Zooker and was working there now but whoever it was, he would know things I needed to know. More importantly, he was probably there alone, since Albertini's was strictly a no-cash stop. People made their bets there, then dropped off an envelope with cash and their number on it at a bar around the corner. If they won, they went to a third location to pick up their winnings. Each location was insulated from the other, and the operators at each supposedly didn't know about the other two.

Since the days of RICO, even the simplest things have gotten more complicated.

A light bell dinged as I stepped through the doorway to Albertini's. Something immediately seemed off about the place, though I couldn't pin down what. The radio still played like it probably always had, filling the air with crooners from the '50s and '60s. I'm sure the Chairman and Dino were high in the rotation. There were two customers, each in a chair manned by small, old Italian men in white coats. A third, who could have been a brother to the first two, slowly and methodically worked a broom around his empty chair.

The fourth chair had a barber sitting in it, reading a skin mag. He was younger than the others, maybe my age. The back of his chair had a nice name-plate, just like the others.

CHARLES, it read.

Shit. I forgot about him.

Last time I'd been here, his name on the chair back was still scrawled in black sharpie on white cardboard. And he'd given me plenty of attitude, too. I solved the problem by driving his own scissors into one of his ass cheeks, and that ended that. Until now.

He didn't bother looking up from his nudie book when I came in, which figured. There was an empty chair ahead of him, and he was still the junior guy in the shop. He'd have to wait for one of the others to kick off before he'd get a promotion, and even then, they might bring in a cousin or something.

I wondered if he still lived with his mother.

The first two barbers didn't pause in their work, but gave me a side-long glance. The one with the broom stopped sweeping, looked up at me, and returned to his sweeping. So much for customer service. I pushed the issue, approaching the sweeper. When I got close enough, I held out a couple of bills that were about double what a haircut cost. He looked up at me again, looked at the money, thought about it, then took it. That surprised me a little, even though it was what I was hoping for. But maybe he figured I was a rube who thought he was who I placed a bet with.

"I need to talk to whoever took Zooker's place," I said. I tried to keep my voice quiet, but despite the radio and the clipper sounds, I knew everyone in the place could hear me. And I sensed everything pause after I spoke. It wasn't a comfortable pause, either.

The old barber pocketed my money. "Zooker gone," he said.

"I know."

Oh, I knew.

The old barber just looked at me.

"Who took his place?" I asked. "Who'd Trepani send in?"

The old barber continued to stare at me as if I were speaking Mandarin.

"*Lei parla inglese?*" I used the formal speech out of respect for his age, hoping it gave me some points with him.

He nodded. "*Sì, certo.* But Zooker? Gone."

"Like I said, I know that. But—"

"Well, well, well. Lookee what we got here." Chuck

had roused himself from his chair. "Never thought I'd see your ugly face in here again."

I ignored him, and focused on the old barber. "Who does that work now? I need to talk to him."

"I've been waiting for this," Chuck said.

Reluctantly, I turned to face him. "You never thought I'd come back, but you were waiting for it? That's brilliant logic, Einstein."

He scowled. "Still a wiseass cunt, huh? Well, things have changed since last time you were here."

"Your mom kicked you out of her basement?"

His face reddened. Christ, he was easy.

"Just leave me alone, Chuck. I've got business here, and then I'll be gone."

He shook his head. "You forgot something last time. I'll get it for you."

He turned and walked away, his limp noticeable as he headed toward the chest of drawers by his chair. Jesus, he was so predictable. He was going to pull out his scissors and come at me with them to even the score. He'd probably even try to stab me in the ass with them, too.

I took the moment while Chuck was rummaging in his drawer to turn back to the old barber. "Just tell me where the new guy is, and I'm gone." I motioned toward the pocket where he'd stashed the money I'd given him. "*Per favore.*"

He shook his head and opened his mouth to speak, but Chuck interrupted. He did it without speaking. The sharp metallic click of a hammer being drawn back echoed through the shop.

I froze. The other barbers froze. Both customers stood, tore off the cutting drapes in one smooth motion, and strode out the door in unison. They couldn't have choreographed it better if they'd tried.

Chuck leered at me. "Not so smart now, are you, bitch?"

I raised my hands to shoulder level. My heart was racing. Sweat popped out at my temples and forehead, and my whole body felt warm. I tried to control my breathing, to force myself calm, but the muzzle of Chuck's revolver looked about three feet in diameter, so it was hard.

But I was definitely living in the moment now.

"Come in here," he muttered, moving toward me. "Acting all tough. Using sneaky little tricks to take advantage of a guy. You think you can get away with that?"

I didn't answer.

He came closer, jabbing the barrel toward me. "Do you?"

I still didn't answer. He was three feet away now, but then he stopped and cocked his head at me. He actually turned the gun sideways, too. "How's it feel, bitch? You like it?"

He was in full-fledged fantasy mode now. I wondered how many times this masturbation-fueled scenario had gone through his mind. If I'd been thinking straighter, I would have realized that was probably the case, and picked a different storefront.

But I was here now. And if there was going to be a later, he needed to come just a little bit closer...

When I didn't give him the answer he wanted, his face screwed up in anger. "Fucking answer me, bitch! Or I'll grease you right here!"

I tried to make my voice sound as calm as I could. Then

I said, "Is 'bitch' the best you can do, you fourth-chair mama's boy?"

His eyes widened and the red left his face, turning white instead. He took another step closer. "I'll fucking kill you, you fucking...twat!" He punctuated both words with a jab of the muzzle.

I glanced around at the barber shop. The other three barbers were watching, disapproval etched in their faces. I wondered suddenly if Chuck were a nephew to one of them, a family albatross foisted upon the business.

"Look at me!" Chuck growled.

I looked back at him. My guts were roiling and my heart was slamming in my chest, but I did my best to project calmness.

Chuck nodded approvingly. "That's right. Look at me, because I'm going to shoot you in the face, bitch."

"In a family place, Chuck?" I shook my head. "I don't think Trepani would approve."

He began to laugh at me. His guffaws were short of maniacal, but he was definitely in on a joke I didn't know. Luckily, I didn't have to wait long to be in on it.

"This ain't no family place no more!" he shouted. "Not like it was. Now it's just a place where people get their fucking haircut."

I glanced over at the old barber who'd been sweeping earlier. He gave me the slightest of nods.

"Don't look at him!" Chuck shouted. "You look at me!"

And he stepped forward, pressing the barrel to my forehead.

Only my forehead wasn't there anymore.

I moved my head left and swept my left hand to the

right, latching onto the wrist of his gun hand. I swiveled my hips toward him and pulled him forward, the direction he was already leaning. Then I clasped his wrist with my right hand. That freed up my left, so I drove my elbow straight back into his face. There was a meaty crunch when the blow landed, and Chuck grunted. His grip loosened, and I stripped the pistol out of his hand.

Stunned, he stood leaning forward, pointing an empty hand and a single finger at nothing. I twisted the opposite direction, whipping the revolver around. I let it swing high and then arc downward, before smashing the butt end into his collar bone.

He squealed in pain. His knees gave out and he flopped to the floor.

I pointed the gun at him. I thought about pumping one into him, or even all six. But I already had two bodies in a Greek diner to worry about. And while I didn't think the cops would make much headway on the case, every bit of damage I did to Trepani only stepped up his efforts to come after me. I preferred him as lackadaisical as possible. Killing Chuck went against that.

I should at least call him a bitch, though, right?

In the end, I took the high road. While Chuck lay on the white tile whimpering, I opened the cylinder to the revolver and let the rounds clatter to the floor around him. Then I tossed the empty pistol to the old barber I'd been talking to before we'd been interrupted.

"No more bets here?" I asked.

He shook his head no.

"Where, then?"

"DeSasso's," he said.

"The pool hall? RACK 'EM UP?"

He nodded.

"I thought he was dead."

"He is."

"So whose place is it now?"

He only shrugged. "I don't pay so much attention any more, *sì*? Not since they move from here."

That made sense. "All right. *Grazie mille, signore.*"

"*Prego.*"

"Tell me something." I nudged Chuck in the ass with the toe of my shoe. He moaned, even though it couldn't have hurt. "Is he..." I started to ask the old barber, but then trailed off. The sad look on his face gave me the answer.

Family.

Was it ever not a burden?

I left without another word, because I knew the answer to that question, too.

FIFTEEN
Cameron

It wasn't enough booze. My arm burned like Vincent was giving me a tattoo with a buzz saw. I wasn't sure how much more I could take. I'd stopped counting at sixteen stitches, but Vincent kept on going and even starting humming to himself at one point. He seemed to enjoy stitching human flesh as much as a nice hemline.

My head swooned and I felt the world tilt to the right. The edges of my vision turned black.

"Woah there," Vincent said. "Maybe we oughta call it quits for now."

"Yeah," I said. "Maybe."

"I got you pretty much squared away anyhow." He snipped the length of black thread and began to tie off a knot. "I tried to keep it straight, make it pretty, y'know?"

"Being pretty isn't really my thing."

"At least maybe you won't have to wear long sleeves every place you go." Snip, he cut the thread. "All done."

My arm looked like an undercooked steak. Red and raw and swollen, the black line of stitches ran like train tracks up my arm, but he was right—the track was straight.

"I really can't thank you enough, Vinny."

He waved a hand and kept putting away his scissors and sewing kit. "Was nothing."

"It wasn't nothing." I tried to slip my arm back through the sleeve of my shirt, but the fabric felt like sandpaper coated in gasoline. I needed a sling. I needed more booze.

"You got something I could make myself a sling with?"

Vincent rose and went behind the curtain. As he stood he stretched out his back with a series of loud pops. He'd been working at my arm for almost an hour, hunched over and concentrating hard. He came shuffling back with a long spool of dark fabric. He got his scissors again and cut a long strip, then helped me tie a cradle for my arm. The pressure of resting it in the sling hurt like hell, but once I got used to it I could tune out the pain for short stretches.

"So what now?" Vincent asked.

I sat there like a dumbass. Good fucking question. I'd been in a mode where I couldn't think more than a few minutes into the future, but now I had to. So, yeah, what was I gonna do?

I told him honestly. "I'm not sure."

"You get him for this," Vincent pointed at my arm. "Fazzio."

I guessed those were my two choices: fight or flight. It didn't seem right to let their attempted murder of me go unanswered, especially given my profession. I also had to consider that if they wanted me dead they weren't going to simply stop because I slipped out on them. If anything I'd pissed them off more. Fazzio Sr. was probably cooling in a hospital somewhere getting a more sanitary job done with his stitches and plotting his revenge.

If I ran, they'd probably follow. Or one night someone like me shows up at the door. No, with this fight they started, I had to finish it.

"I hate to ask another favor...," I said.

"What is it?"

"Can I use your phone?"

"Of course." Vincent reached under the counter and pulled out a large black phone still connected by a cord to the wall. I didn't know these things still existed. It had buttons, not a rotary dial, but the thing was still an antique.

"I'll give you privacy," he said and went back into the apartment he shared with his wife.

I lifted the receiver off the cradle and stared at the numbers. I wanted to call Bricks but it sunk into me right then that I had no idea what her number was. I had it stored on my cell and all I ever did was hit the letter B in my address book and it came up. Goddamn technology.

I couldn't tell her I was okay. I couldn't warn her about Fazzio mentioning her name. I didn't know if she was okay at all. If they came after me, chances are they went after her too. Although between the two of us, I'd give her better odds no matter who was on her trail.

I did know one number by heart. Tia. I checked the clock on the wall. A little after nine-thirty, not too late to call. At least I wouldn't piss her off or send her into a panic, so I dialed.

"Hello?"

"It's me."

I didn't expect her to bust out in song, but she barely seemed happy to hear from me at all. My suspicions about our second chance relationship were being confirmed, but I didn't have time to sort out that mess.

"How are you?"

"Fine, I guess." How to explain what my little trip to Boston had become. "Things went a little sideways, to tell you the truth."

"Sideways how?" I wanted concern for me and my

safety, but she wanted to know how I'd screwed up another job. I never told her the details of my work, never told her my nickname—Slaughterhouse. She already disapproved of my job so I didn't need to rub it in.

"Just some complications," I said, trying to minimize the damage. "I'm going to be here an extra couple days."

"What happened?" No *Come home, baby, please don't leave me alone.*

"Boston hasn't exactly been a hospitable town."

"What do you mean?"

"Let's just say I won't be rooting for the Patriots any time soon."

"Cam," Tia sounded exhausted. "Are you in danger?"

"No, baby. Not a bit."

She sighed like my lie had been a failure, but she didn't press the point. She'd given up. Given up on me. When I got back I'd let her know she wasn't obliged to stay with me just because I'd helped her with that jerk-off boyfriend of hers. I needed to let her go, let her know I already knew she was one foot out the door.

"Do me a favor. Did I ever leave Bricks' number around your place?"

"She's not with you?"

"No. And I need to get in touch with her. So, did I tell you her number?"

"No, why would I have it?" There was a bite of angry jealousy there, perhaps.

"You wouldn't. Just had to try."

"Where are you staying up there? Are you safe?"

"I'll be fine." I heard Vincent moving around behind the curtain. "I'm with family."

"Your aunt?"

I almost said, "What aunt?" then I remembered—I did have an aunt in Boston. Maybe a great aunt or an aunt once removed, but she was family. Of course, all the family I'd met so far up here wanted to kill me...

"Yeah. Aunt Ruby. How'd you remember?"

"I don't know. I heard you mention her."

Mixed signals. She sounds like she can't wait for me to be out of her life, or that she wouldn't shed a tear if someone told her tomorrow I'd been shot, but then she remembers small details. She wants to know if I'm safe, a little late in the conversation, but still.

"I'll be home in a few days." Now it's me who's rushing her off the line so I can call Aunt Ruby.

"Take care of yourself, Cam."

"I will. Thanks."

There was an awkward pause while each of us waited to see if this call with end with a hollow I love you. It didn't and we hung up.

Vincent came back into the shop. "So?"

I know it's there so I asked him, "Do you have a phone book?"

Vincent reached under his desk like it's a magic trick and produced another antique—the last remaining white pages in North America. And goddamn if the thing doesn't still have her number.

Before I can call Vincent asked me, "So you're gonna get him?"

I did my best to put on an appropriate face for someone in my line of work. "Yeah. I am."

Vincent smiled. He took my hand in his and turned it palm up, then he slid me a tiny two-shot Remington. It was a boot gun, a slip-in-the-sock kind of weapon. Small, tiny caliber, only enough ammo that you'd better be right on top of your target, and with power like this thing had you'd better be barrel-to-the-temple close.

"Vincent, I can't."

"You take it." He closed my fingers around the gun. "I see you don't have one with you. And don't say a damn thing to my wife about it." He glanced over his shoulder just in case.

"Thank you."

"You get that bastard," he said.

"I'll try."

SIXTEEN
Bricks

Tony DeSasso used to own the RACK 'EM UP, a bar and billiards place that was really just another family storefront. Before him, it was a straight establishment owned by a couple of brothers named Domini, and some people still called it that even after they sold out to the mob. I'd bet it was one-stop shopping back when DeSasso ran things. I'd never been, but even in the circles I traveled in, I'd heard of it. It was one of those places where if you walked in and saw the freaks from the *Star Wars* cantina scene playing music and shooting nine ball, you'd just nod carefully, do your dirty little business and leave. No questions, and no talking about it afterward.

The sign outside was new. Well, kind of new. The place was called RACKS 11 now, but they'd recycled the RACK part of the original sign, slapping on the S and the 11. Those parts of the sign were newer and cleaner, with brighter bulbs and less city grime to dim them. Whoever owned the place now wasn't fooling anyone.

It wasn't Tony DeSasso, I knew. Cam made sure of that, back right before we met. So someone new took over, changed the sign, and then what? Made nice with Trepani, and business as usual? Probably.

But what the hell did RACKS 11 mean?

From the looks of the place, the sign was about all that was changed. When Cam told me the story of the DeSasso hit, he aptly described the RACK 'EM UP as a shit stain on the sidewalk. Well, it still was.

I stood outside for about forty minutes, scoping the place out. There was a fair amount of traffic in and out during that time, more along the lines of a bodega than a pool hall. There was definitely action happening inside. Which was good, and bad.

Good because I'd find what I wanted, which was Trepani's people.

Bad for the same reason.

I watched the place for another fifteen minutes, sipping on a soda from a hot dog stand. Traffic continued, unabated. Jesus, how did the cops not know about this place?

I shook my head at my own stupid question. Of course they knew.

While I watched, I checked my cell for the tenth time. Nothing from Cam.

When my soda was empty, I tossed the can into the trash, took a deep cleansing breath, and headed toward the pool hall. Time to get some answers.

I pushed open the door, and strode inside. The first thing I noticed was the smell. You'd think with all the in and out traffic, the place would be well ventilated, but it wasn't. The air was stuffy, and filled with cigarette and cigar smoke, stale beer, old sweat, and the weak odor of bleach in the background.

The smoke is the only thing that surprised me. Smoking indoors was against city ordinances now, and had been for years. But I guess when you're running a front for the mob, you don't worry about the EPA or whoever enforces that law. You just say fuck it, and fire up the cancer sticks.

Nice. I'd never get the smell out. I'd have to burn my clothes after.

No one took any notice of me, at least not outwardly. But I could feel the sidelong glances. I wasn't their usual clientele, and anything unusual got noticed. The trick was to become usual, and the key to that was to act as if you belonged. So I walked to the bar without breaking stride, trying to radiate confidence.

The bartender was the only one actually looking at me dead on. When I sat down, he sidled down the bar to stand in front of me. He was skinny guy with a prominent Adam's apple, and looking at him, my clichéd brain went straight to Ichabod Crane.

"Getchya?" His phrasing was sharp, but his words ran together like a mumble.

"What's on tap?" I asked.

"Whudelse? Bud."

"Light?"

He gave me a queer look. "You kiddin' me? You see anyone in here wants to watch their girlish figure?"

That was a perfect excuse to look around the place without seeming suspicious, so I did just that. Despite all the traffic through the place, there weren't many actual customers. A pair of goombahs were shooting pool at the middle table, acting like they weren't watching everything. When one leaned down for a shot, I saw the flash of silver underneath his arm. Down at the end of the bar, a lonely looking prostitute sat, fiddling with the straw in her drink. Closer to me, but still five chairs away, a fat mouth breather with a shaved head hunkered over a beer and a shot. He was doing the best job of anyone in the place of pretending to ignore me, but I could feel his attention all the same.

Aside from that, a couple of young kids were shooting pool on the far table. Best as I could tell, they were likely the only true customers in the place, but I was basing that largely on the fact that one was Puerto Rican and the other black. Even these days, the family was pretty strict about being Italian to be part of the business. If you weren't Italian, you'd better be white, and married to an Italian, like my pops. Otherwise, the most you could hope for was the equivalent of entry-level, minimum wage work.

But who knows? Trepani spent a lot of time in Florida. Maybe he broadened his horizons down there, and decided to make his family more of a rainbow coalition. Those two could be the ones handling the dope traffic.

I turned back to the bartender. "I guess not."

"So? Whatullitbe?"

"Beer's fine." I laid a ten on the bar.

He moved a few feet away, selecting a glass from behind the bar.

"Hey, what's RACKS 11 mean?" I asked, partly because I wanted to build a little rapport, but also because I was curious. "Is that a pool term, or...?"

"Inside joke," he said while he drew me a glass that was almost a third foam.

"What's the joke?"

He finished drawing the beer, but didn't knock off any of the head. He put the glass down in front of me. "Like I said, it's an inside joke. If I toldya, itudbe an outside joke."

So much for building rapport.

When he reached for the ten dollar bill, I put my hand over it and gave him a hard look. "You kiddin' me?"

"What?"

"There's more head on this than a Saturday night out on the stroll."

He smiled slightly, showing me small, feral teeth. "Heh. That's pretty funny."

I pushed the beer back toward him with my free hand. "Fix it."

His smile hardened to a scowl, but he took my beer and returned to the tap. There, he made a big show of filling it to the absolute lip, stopping and letting the foam recede before adding more. He cast me a couple of sarcastic glances while he worked. When he came back and slid the drink toward me, there was only a skim of white foam on the top. It jiggled and splashed over the edges of the glass and onto the bar.

"Good'nuff?"

"Thank you," I made sure to draw the ten-spot through the spillage before handing it to him. "And keep it."

He didn't know how to react, since my response and the generous tip had to be giving him mixed emotions. He settled for keeping the scowl in place, took the ten, and set about ignoring me like everyone else in the place.

Well, almost everyone.

It only took the wheezing mouth breather about two minutes before he moved down the bar toward me. He took the stool next to me without asking. "Can't blame the guy, really."

"Who, him?" I motioned toward the bartender.

"Yeah. You can't blame Icky."

"Icky? His name is actually Icky?" I looked to see if the

bartender had a nametag or something. That would have been too much to hope for, but still...Icky?

"Yeah," the mouth breather said. "That's his nickname. It's short for Ichabod, on account of he looks like that fucking guy in the cartoon with the headless ghost guy on the horse."

There are times in this world when you feel like you're slipping. Like maybe your brain is getting a little flabby. I'm here to tell you, when you start making intellectual associations that are the same ones attributed by people only slighter smarter than lichens? Yeah, that is definitely one of those times.

I needed to read more.

Clearly.

"Anyway," he said, "You can't blame Icky for the beer, right?"

"How's that?"

"Well, what I mean is, he takes one look at you, and all he wants to do is give you a lot of head."

I stared at him in disbelief. He had just uttered what had to be the worst pick up line I'd ever heard.

He raised both hands in mock surrender. "Hey, I'm just sayin'. I mean, it's a perfectly natural reaction." He smiled, his thick sausage lips stretching into a thinly disguised leer.

I turned away in disgust.

That didn't deter him. "Man sees you?" He snapped his fingers. "First thing that comes to mind is eating pussy."

I took a drink of my beer while he waited for me to respond. I knew I couldn't just ignore him and hope he went away. He was already in too far for that. So I turned back to him and said, "Is that supposed to be a pick up line? Because I'm not interested."

He wagged those fingers at me again in that oddly familiar way. "See, there's the rub. Because I'm wondering something. I'm wondering, does a man think about eating pussy when he sees you 'cause that's what he wants to do? Or is it all, like, subsexual, and shit?"

"Subsexual? Are you kidding me?"

"No, I'm a hunnerd percent serious. Is it something subsexual that he picks up on?"

"I have no idea what you're talking about, so let's just—"

He ignored me, continuing. "Maybe he picks up on all that because, you know, down in all that subsexual unnerstanding, he can tell it's you who wants to eat pussy."

That stopped me. Between the finger wagging and this, I was starting to suspect something. I looked closer at his face, really examining his features.

They were close. Not exact, but close.

"I'm sorry," I said. "I didn't catch your name?"

"I didn't give it to you. Not a lot of names get exchanged in this place, y'know?"

"What's yours?"

His smile grew a little, but there was no humor in it, only a dark, joyful malevolence. "Tell you what. We'll do like that Lecter movie. Squid for crow, right?"

I blinked, then got it.

Quid pro quo.

Christ. I was dealing with a complete retard.

But the caginess in his eyes belied that. I didn't know if he screwed up the movie line on purpose or he really thought he quoted it right, but it didn't matter. He wasn't a patron here. He was working, and if he was working here, he knew how to do his job. He probably had a goddamn PhD in it. So I had to be careful not to equate ignorance with stupidity.

"Fine," I agreed. "What's your name?"

He shook his head. "No, ladies first." He leaned in a little bit and lowered his voice. "Here's my first question. You think Icky saw you and wanted to chow down? Or did he figure he wasn't the only one in the place with a liquor...sorry, a *lick her* license?"

I glanced at the bartender, who was busying himself wiping the same spot on the bar and pretending to watch the pool game. Then I looked back at my deranged conversation partner. "What I think, the last time Icky got laid, Clinton was still in charge."

He chuckled insincerely. "Not exactly an answer, but since you're probably right, I'll let that one pass." He waved his hand at me. "Go ahead. Your turn."

"What's your name?" I asked, but I knew what the answer would be, or at least part of it.

"Vito," he said proudly. "Vito Taggliarti."

I stared at him, forcing my expression impassive. "Well, nice to meet you, Vito," I said calmly. I switched hands on my beer, cupping the glass with my left and freeing my right as if to shake his hand.

His hands remained still, but his smile faded a little. "You don't recognize the name? Aw, come on. Bruno was my cousin. You remember Bruno, right?"

I nodded slowly. "I remember him."

"He knew you, too. The famous Bricks. Can't even begin to tell you how happy he was to be your handler when that happened. Proudest day of his life." Vito fixed me with a stare. "He do all right by you?"

I hesitated, measuring my words. "He made himself clear," I finally said.

Vito chuckled, only this time I thought at least part of that laugh was real. "Oh, he was good at that, huh?" His chuckle faded away quickly, and he asked me, "You know he got killed? Shot down in the street like a dog."

"I heard."

"You heard? You..." He shook his head. "Oh, that's good. You heard."

I thought about offering my condolences, but I was getting the strong feeling that play time was almost over, so I remained silent. For his part, Vito looked down into his beer, shaking his head some more. Then he took a long swig, let out a deep breath, followed with a small belch.

"She heard," he muttered, and took another drink.

My mind was buzzing with possibilities. I knew that without a doubt Vito was armed. I'd seen for sure that one of the pool players was, and the other one had to be, too. The bartender might have something behind the bar, and the two kids playing pool could be packing as well. So a minimum of three on one, maybe as much as six on one.

Long odds.

Vito turned slowly on his stool until he was facing me. "This is a dirty business," he said, his tone full of insincere regret. "Anyone who gets into it, runs a risk. I know the risk, they know the risk—" he pointed in the general direction of the pool players "—and Bruno knew the risk. High risk, high reward. Sometimes you get the reward, sometimes the risk gets you. That's what happened to

Bruno. The risk got him. And I'm at peace with that. Really, I am."

I didn't believe him, but I didn't have an answer, either, so I settled for shifting in my seat and moving my hand just a couple of inches closer to my purse. It might not matter in the end, but then again, sometimes inches and fractions of a second do matter. A lot.

"See, though," Vito continued, "the part that bothers me is the mystery of it. The wondering, y'know? I mean, I got curiosity and it's like an itch that I can't scratch." He brought his hand up to his face and scratched the stubble there, as if to illustrate his point. "Maybe you can help me. It's your turn, after all. Squid for crow, and all that shit."

I nodded slowly, and motioned to him with my right hand. "Sure," I said evenly. When I put my hand back down, it was at the edge of bar, that much closer to the .45 in the side pocket of my purse.

He smiled, still touching his face. "Aw, I'm full of shit. It's not that I'm really too curious about it, but goddamned if Bruno wasn't. I mean, he'd have to be, to even tell me about it, right?"

"Tell you what?" I asked, but by now I had an idea.

He pulled his hand away, turning up the palm in front of him. "It's a simple thing. The question is, are you a dyke, or what?"

I had flashes of all the times Bruno Taggliarti, one of Sal's bodyguards, asked me that question. How he hammered on it. I had no idea why he cared, but the indignity of the question always pissed me off. I fired back at him with barbs, which was part of the fun for that fat fuck. And then he'd come back at me with the same question again, just framed slightly differently. It was an obsession for him, probably right up until the moment I put a bullet in his eye on the street outside Cazulli's diner.

Vito's black grin didn't waver, but his eyes hardened with a killer's intensity. I thought about making the first move. Action is faster than reaction, I told myself. The stuffy air in the place was electric with danger now, and Icky the bartender wiped his way further down the bar. Pool balls clacked in the background, and for the first time, I realized there was rock and roll music playing quietly over the pool hall's sound system. Santana's "Black Magic Woman" was going to be the soundtrack for whatever fight played out in the next few moments. I didn't believe in fate or in signs, but either way, I hoped Carlos and his guitar licks brought me some positive karma.

"You gonna solve the mystery?" Vito asked quietly, his voice lower and meaner than before. Then he glanced over my shoulder at the door, and his face brightened. He looked back at me. "Come on, tell the truth." He pointed a thick index finger over my shoulder. "You'd fuck her, right?"

I glanced involuntarily in the direction he pointed, knowing I'd made a mistake before my chin even reach my shoulder. I turned back, plunging my hand into my purse. Just as my fingertips found the cold metal of my .45, Vito's fist hammered into my jaw. I'm sure I flew backward off that barstool, my arms and legs splayed outward like a human airplane, but like a red-eye to JFK, I slept through the entire flight, including the landing.

SEVENTEEN
Cameron

Aunt Ruby slapped me across the face.

"Of course I know who you are," she said, then she grabbed the same cheek she'd just hit and kissed it, leaving a smear of lipstick in her namesake shade.

"I haven't seen you since you was three feet high and used to drive all them toys cars around the carpet." She spoke in a thick never-left-Boston accent that sounded like the letter R had been stricken from the English language. "Me and your ma used to be able to talk for hours while you played with them cars. How is your ma, anyway?"

I didn't have the heart to tell her Mom stopped talking to me years ago when I went in to the family business. "She's fine," I lied.

"Aw, you're such a bullshitter." Ruby smiled at me, showing yellow teeth with wide gaps between. Her wrinkled skin flapped when she talked, her hands never not moving. Her jewelry clanked on her wrist and around her neck. Thick gold bracelets and necklaces with chunky fake rubies in each. She really took the name to heart.

"I really appreciate you taking me in like this," I said.

"Of course, of course. You're family." Family she hadn't seen or heard from in two decades, but blood ran thick around these parts. It could get you taken in to a practical stranger's house in Ruby's case, or in Fazzio's case it could get you killed.

She finally noticed my arm.

"What the hell happened to you?"

Aunt Ruby was what they used to call brassy. She told it like she saw it, your feelings be damned. She was loud, still dyed her hair a jet black, and wore all that hardware even though her bones looked too frail to hold it all up. Her voice was raspy from a half century of cigarette smoking and her back was slightly hunched in a permanent stoop. Still, I wouldn't want to piss her off. She just gave off that kind of vibe.

"I ran into some trouble."

"Some trouble? You look like you ran into a friggin' chainsaw."

She took my arm and pushed up the fabric of my sling until she could see the stitching. Bolts of pain shot through me, but I held my tongue.

"Jesus Christ on horseback," she said. "Lemme guess—shaving accident."

She showed me those rotten teeth again. I grinned a toothless smile, hoped it would inspire her to do the same. I gently slid the sling back in place, flexing my fingers as I did to get a little of the blood back into them. With my sleeve rolled out of the way up to my biceps it acted like a blood pressure cuff and my arm had started to go numb.

"Just a guy I had some words with. It's kinda why I'm here."

"Sit, sit," she said. We were in her living room. Decorations—circa 1981. She had a record player, a TV with a set of rabbit ears on top, and a sofa with plastic seat covers. If she lived in Brooklyn she'd be the ultimate hipster. I sat on the couch with a creak of plastic sheeting. She sat next to me.

I said, "I'm trying to get back in touch with the men who did this."

"Why? So they can finish the job?"

"No. So I can pay them back."

She patted my knee and her bracelets rattled. "Good, boy. My Arthur, God rest him," she paused to cross herself, "he never took shit from no one. Anyone did that to him," she pointed at my arm. "Tried to unzip his skin right offa him? He'd have their balls in a vice. Or, shit, he'd cut them off and bring them home to me so I could fry them up and add them to the sauce."

Like I said—brassy.

"I know it's been a while since Uncle Arthur has been around, but I wonder if you still know a lot of people in the neighborhood."

"Shit, I know everyone. Don't go thinking Arthur was the brains behind his business. He had the balls, but I had the smarts." She said it *smaahts.* I cringed.

"Do you know the Fazzios?"

Her mouth turned down into a frown. Her hand started moving in an upside-down claw with her fingers all pinched together. I couldn't interpret the exact motion, but I could tell it wasn't a happy gesture.

"A Fazzio done this to you?"

"Yeah," I said.

"Those mother—" And here her voice rose to a shrill screech. "—FUCKERS!"

Aunt Ruby was up and moving now, pacing the floor like a heavyweight before a fight.

"Fuckin' Fazzio has been a boil on the ass of this city for too fuckin' long."

"I've been to his office, but I wanted to know if there

was someplace a little less obvious I could find him. Like someplace I wouldn't be met at the door with a gun before a hello."

Aunt Ruby was barely listening to me. "Fazzio done it?" she asked again, but rhetorically. "He cuts up my family? My cousin's little boy, he cuts in two."

"So, do you know where I can find him?"

Ruby clapped her hands together. "I'll do you one better. I'll get you two escorts."

Ruby's sons Tag and Boyd were street-raised and street-wise. They were a matched set of muscle bound greasers. Buzz cuts, tank tops, track pants and what seemed like a compulsion to keep scratching at their balls like they were constantly fighting off a case of the crabs.

"They'll take you right to him, the fuck," Aunt Ruby said. "Boys, this is your cousin, Cameron."

"Third cousin or something," I said. "Twice removed maybe, I don't know."

"Who gives a shit?" asked Ruby. "Family is family."

The boys were my age but projected a much younger image. I could tell they were untested. Bar fights and brawls outside a Bruins' game didn't really make them qualified to go after big game like Fazzio, but I was more than happy to have some muscle with me.

We shook hands. "Thanks for helping me out, guys."

"No problem," Tag said.

"The guy's a douche," Boyd said.

"So you know where we could hit him?" I asked.

"Him and his guys hang out at a couple different places."

We'd start at one and work our way down the list. First stop, a seedy bar in Kenmore Square. After Tag parked the car they each gave a two fingered salute to the shadow of Fenway Park and went to the trunk to retrieve two sawed off hockey sticks to be used like clubs. Nothing for me, but I had Vincent's mini-gun. Lucky for me, a bar is ripe with improvised weapons. And if I knew Fazzio's crew at all—and I think I did after the beating they gave me—I'd be able to grab one of their weapons once the first guy was down.

To be at least a little more ready, I slid the sling off my arm, tested it a few times and didn't scream from the pain so I figured it would do me fine if I needed it.

"This fucker really do that to your arm?" Tag asked.

"His father, actually."

"No shit?"

"No shit. He was in the act of pushing me out a window at the time."

"Told you," Boyd said. "Douche."

We made a lap of the bar, checking every dark corner, but no Fazzio. We left and I was glad to be out of the place and away from the terrible bar band whose singer sounded like she swallowed a rabid weasel and gyrated like the ghost of Stevie Nicks was trying to escape her body.

"You sure you boys can find him?" I worried.

"Boston's a small town," Tag said.

He proved his point when we drove back over to the North End in the time it would take me to get a car out of a parking lot in New York. Next stop, a spaghetti joint with red and white checked table cloths and Chianti bottles dripping with candle wax on every table.

People gave us a slanted eye as we walked with purpose around the room, Tag and Boyd brandishing their hockey stubs like hunters, which is what we were, basically.

No Fazzio.

Next up was a more upscale bar a few blocks away. It was close enough to the water that I could smell the rot of seaweed mixed with fuel from the docks and hear the occasional squawk of seagulls.

Tag put his hand on his forehead to shade the glass from the street light glare as he peered in the window. "There he is."

I stepped behind him to look. Fazzio was at the bar with his two beefy sidekicks beside him. Fazzio Sr. wasn't there. Charlie, the one who'd dented my nose, was listening to Fazzio tell some story and as I checked out the sheer size of him and his counterpart, I looked back to Tag and Boyd. They were strong, sure, but not like Charlie and friend. But they were all I had.

"All right, fellas," I said. "Leave Fazzio for me."

My two cousins high fived and let out a whoop like you'd hear at a Sox game when someone hit a homer. They tightened their grips on the hockey sticks and I let them go first into the fight. I spotted an empty bar stool at the first spot inside the door. That seat was mine. Not for sitting. For using the metal legs to crack some fucking skulls.

EIGHTEEN
Bricks

I've been knocked out exactly twice in my entire life.

Both times by men.

Both times, those men were mobsters.

Both times, I came to suddenly and clearly.

Both times, when I woke up, I was tied up.

The world is full of coincidences.

This time, my wrists were bound to the back of the chair with what felt like shoelaces. I couldn't have been sitting there too long because I could still feel my hands, and the knots felt tight enough to cut off circulation. The tips of my fingers throbbed in protest.

Worse than that, the pain in my head banged and pulsed in counterpoint to the finger throbbing. Vito had clocked me good, right on the jaw. I could feel the stiffness in the skin and the warmth there, so I knew my face was swelling up. If I got out of this one, I'd probably look like Stallone at the end of *Rocky*.

Getting out. That had to be my priority.

I glanced around the small room. The lights were out but the darkness was more of a grayness. Light leaked in from under the door, and from a small rectangular window up high. I think the window led out to the alley behind the pool hall. My eyes didn't take long to adjust further, and I scanned the room for an exit. The window was way too small, and the door no doubt led right back into the lion's den, so neither of them were any good. I tried to spot another door, maybe one that led out to that alley, but all I saw was junk stacked against the walls, and walls.

Only my hands were secured to the chair, so my feet were free. But when I tried move, I discovered immediately that the chair was bolted to the floor.

Uh-oh.

That was no accident. Bolting a chair to the floor is a purposeful act. Vito and whoever else ran this place had used this chair and this room for things like this before. That didn't bode well for me.

A shadow broke the slice of light coming underneath the door. When the shadow remained still for a few moments, then shifted to my right again, I realized what it was. Someone was standing guard. Vito? Probably not. But regardless who it was, I knew I didn't have a lot of time. For all I knew, Vito was making sure he had enough shovels and lime to take care of my body, or looking for a nice construction site about to pour cement.

Think!

I tugged at the laces holding my wrists, but there was no play there. I pushed again with my feet, trying to move the chair, but it didn't budge.

There are always options, I told myself. Think!

My legs and feet were free. That was my greatest advantage. But how to use that advantage? Timing was critical. And positioning. And if Vito were smart—

I stopped. That was my greatest advantage. I was smarter than that motherfucker. He was street-wise and cagey, maybe even more so than me. But in the end, I knew I was smarter, and I had to find a way to press that advantage.

How?

I could get him mad. Rip on his cousin Bruno, tell how I shot him in the eye and spit on his corpse. Maybe then he'd make a mistake. Come close enough to use my legs on him.

I thought about that, but I couldn't be sure. What if taunting didn't enrage him? What if it just added to that cold fury he already seemed to possess? That would make things worse, not necessarily create an opening.

What else?

I wasn't going to beg, I told myself. At least not for real. But what if I feigned begging? Played the weak female part, weeping and pleading for mercy? That might get him close enough. Might give me a fighting chance.

Another shadow blocked out the light under the door. I heard muffled voices, but could only make out a few words, and none of them made any sense. Then one of the voices raised a little, and suddenly I could hear everything he said.

"I know what he fucking said," Vito barked.

A muffled reply.

"And I won't," Vito snapped back. "But I'm the one what spotted her in the first place. And I'm the one whose cousin she wasted. So I got privileges here."

The tone of the reply seemed beseeching, but I could hear the subtle undertone of submission, even without hearing the words.

Vito laughed. "Soon. Real soon. But don't worry. I got it all handled."

I heard the sound of someone clapping someone else on the shoulder, and then the door swung open. Vito's big, round silhouette filled the doorway. He closed the door behind him and hit the lights.

I blinked against the sudden brightness. As my eyes adjusted, Vito strolled past me and rummaged in a desk drawer. When he found whatever he was looking for, he stepped up behind me and grabbed a handful of my hair. With a jerk, he pulled my head backward so I was staring up at him. His jowly face was even uglier upside down. He'd missed small patches of whiskers the last time he shaved, and there was a clot of something disgusting in one of his hair-choked nostrils. Nostrils that looked like shotgun barrels from the vantage point I had.

Then something glinted off to the side. He brought the knife into full view, ticking it slightly from side to side. His face stretched into a malevolent leer.

"So what do you think, Bricks? Huh? You fucking cunt."

I didn't answer. The harsh light from the bulbs overhead danced off of the silver blade in his hand.

"No smart ass comeback?" Vito said, his tone mock-mournful. "I'm disappointed. Bruno said you were good with that tongue. Probably 'cause of the whole dyke thing, my guess."

My entire body was rigid. I racked my brain for some kind of play, but got nothing but blankness. All I could do was stare at that knife.

"So maybe that's where I'll start," Vito told me, dipping the point of the blade toward my mouth. "Cut out that sharp little tongue of yours? Or maybe a tit? That'd be good, huh?" The knife drifted up along my face. "Or an eye. That might be the best place to get thing rolling. Slice that fucker right up like a stew onion."

Think! I screamed inside.

The only reply came from Vito. "Tell you what, champ. I'm a gentleman here, so we'll do this: you decide. You tell me where to start cutting."

NINETEEN
Cameron

As I lifted the stool I thought to myself: what the hell are you doing?

Revenge wasn't really my thing, and this hadn't been planned out at all. I was going in with two guys I barely knew after a trio of men I definitely knew to be hard asses and out for my blood. Then again, in the life I chose, the option to do nothing isn't really a choice. If you turn the other cheek you can get a shard of glass slashed across it.

Fazzio wanted me dead and running would only make him more annoyed when he had to come after me. I could be found. I'm not in the CIA, for fuck's sake. It was a lot like the situation we faced with Sal. In order to escape I had to burn the whole damn thing down.

Whether that was doable at all or even slightly advisable remained to be seen. In any case I approached Fazzio and his two sides of beef behind Tag and Boyd.

Tag struck first, pounding the back of the muscle man closest to us. The hockey stick cracked between the man's shoulder blades and he toppled forward knocking into Fazzio. Charlie was already turning around and I saw his hand go into his jacket for some firepower. Boyd's stick caught him on the arm and Charlie's gun clattered to the floor.

A woman screamed, chairs scraped across the floor. I followed up behind Tag and swung my barstool down toward the man sliding off Fazzio. He acted as a buffer between me and my main target, but with my thumping shot to the man's back he crumpled and fell faster than he had been, leaving Fazzio exposed. I saw recognition flash across his face as he retreated and reached for his own gun. I pulled hard on the heavy stool and tried to lift it over my head again, my wounded arm buckling under the weight. A nine millimeter would be much easier to lift.

Tag slammed his stick into Fazzio's shoulder, halting his progress in retrieving his gun. Charlie was still up and he took a good old fashioned roundhouse swing at Boyd and caught my cousin with a fist to the side of the head. Boyd reeled and his body fell against the bar.

Around us patrons rushed for the door, one man with a drink still clutched in his hand, his wife still holding her sloshing glass of red wine. Behind the bar the owner started shouting in Italian.

Fazzio had recovered and made another reach for his gun. He was too far away from me to reach so I threw the stool at him, one-handed. It bounced off the forearm he had to put up to block. The chrome legs banged against bone and I heard him grunt over the Dean Martin soundtrack.

I bent down and pawed at the fallen man in search of his gun. I felt a bulge under his jacket, but he was laying on top of it. Above me, Tag swung his hockey stick at Charlie who dodged it. Boyd came off the bar rail and swept his stick at Charlie's face. Charlie reached out and clamped down his enormous hand on the stick, stopping it in midair with a slap. He twisted and wrenched it from Boyd's hand, then turned and cracked it over his skull. The stick splintered and Boyd went down, landing on top of the man I was attempting to overturn, adding more dead weight to my task.

Tag bent down and picked up Charlie's gun off the floor. His face seemed panicked. Holding the sawed off hockey stick had seemed like second nature, but holding a gun frightened him. I didn't want him to have to know what it was like to pull that trigger while aiming at another man.

"Give it here," I said.

Tag stared wide-eyed at Charlie as the bigger man squared himself. I knew he could see the fear in Tag's eyes too. The quick glint of a blade cut the air between them. Charlie had a few tricks up his sleeve even if he'd let his gun get away. Now it became a test of wills between the two men who had the guts to use their weapon first.

I abandoned my hunt for the other gun and stood quickly. Lucky for me, too, because Fazzio had his pistol out and his shot missed me by only inches.

"Give me the gun," I said to Tag. Not only did I not want him to use it, things were looking increasingly like he wasn't going to be able to anyway. Charlie tensed to lunge with his knife as I put my body between him and Tag. I knew I wouldn't have time to grab the gun and turn it on Charlie so I settled for being a blocker. I spun a half turn and felt Charlie's knife sink into my side right below my ribs. The tip broke skin and I felt every fraction of an inch of the blade as it dove below the surface. My skin sparkled in pain, the muscles were ripped and sent shockwaves through me, parts of my gut I couldn't name made themselves aware by the sharp stabs of pain they sent to my brain.

Even worse was the blade pulling out.

Tag's eyes were on mine as my face contorted. I put a hand over the gun and he let it go. I rotated, more of a half fall, and fired at Charlie. Over his shoulder I could see Fazzio trying to get a shot at me past his wide brute of a man.

I hit Charlie in the chest and he turned in on himself. I could tell by the weight of the gun I was holding a full clip—well, minus one now. I didn't stop at Charlie. I fired over his shoulder at Fazzio, but the shot went high. Fazzio continued his retreat.

I spun a quarter turn and shot the man on the ground, careful not to hit Boyd who was coming around. I lifted the gun again and shot Charlie once more in the chest. By then Fazzio was on the run.

I followed his retreat with a series of misplaced shots that chipped the brick on the back wall of the restaurant, smashed into a poster for the movie *Roman Holiday* and took out a set of olive oil and balsamic bottles.

The clip wasn't empty yet, but I was spent. It felt like my whole side had been zippered open as wide as my arm, even though I knew I'd suffered only a puncture.

I had to let Fazzio make it out the back. My arm couldn't even hold the gun anymore.

I felt Tag and Boyd each put a shoulder under my armpit and start to walk me out. To no one they kept saying, "Holy shit, holy shit, holy shit."

I checked over my shoulder at my handiwork. Two down, but the big game got away. Less of a bloodbath than usual for me and for the first time, most of the blood was mine.

TWENTY
Bricks

I stared up at the knife in Vito's hand, his words barely registering. I knew this job was dangerous, but I always thought I'd beat the odds. If I somehow didn't, I figured I'd get it during a straight up fight. Fall in battle, that sort of thing.

Instead, I was tied to a chair with a knife-wielding lunatic debating about where to start cutting on me. I was going to end up in pieces, scattered around the city in dumpsters and sewers. Or hell, they'd probably dissolve the body parts in acid.

"What's it to be, Bricks?" Vito asked, tilting the knife. His hard eyes were full of anticipation.

This is the moment panic sets in, I thought. This was when I'd scream and cry and plead, even though I swore I never would. I'd give this fucker exactly what he wanted, and I'd end up dead anyway. It seemed like an inexorable force, this scenario, and I saw it clearly, as if it happened to someone else, a long time ago and in a very distant place.

But the panic never came.

I felt it flutter loudly in the pit of my stomach, like the first puff of the flame that ignites a forest fire, but then it foundered and went out. Instead, a surreal emptiness surrounded me. It wasn't peaceful, necessarily, but it was calm. I wondered for a second if I was dying. If Vito had already slit my throat and I was bleeding out and just didn't know it yet. But no, there was the knife, shifting in the light before me, while his ugly, deranged face was still in the background. There was no blood on the blade, either, so he hadn't used it yet.

The calmness spread outward through my whole body until it enveloped every part of me. I didn't know how to label it, and at that moment, I didn't care. There'd be time to decide later if it was a warrior's mindset or simple acceptance, if there was a later. But for now, my mind suddenly seemed to be working again, and I made a decision.

"Maybe you should start by cutting your own dick off," I said to him in an even tone.

Vito's eyes bulged in surprise.

"If you can find it," I added.

The leer turned into a snarl. "Oh, I am gonna start with that fucking tongue of yours," he said.

"There's a mirror in my purse," I told him, "if you think that'll help. That little wee-wee's got to be under all that fat somewhere, right?"

The hand with the knife fell toward me, but it was the butt end that struck my cheek. Flashes of white streaked across blackness, but I shook my head and stayed conscious.

"You like that?" Vito asked. He let go of my hair and moved around to the side of my chair. "Get used to it. You're going to feel a lot of it for the rest of your short fucking life."

"What about your life, Vito? Or are you too stupid to see it?"

His eyes narrowed. "Don't you call me stupid, you twat."

"If the shoe fits."

His left shoulder dropped. A split second later, pain erupted in my side. Something between a grunt and a cry escaped my lips. Even through the pain, I had to give the son of a bitch credit. He knew how to punch.

"How's that fit?" he mocked.

I caught my breath, and swallowed. Goddamn, that hurt.

He leaned menacingly over me, swishing the knife back and forth.

"You remember Abe Fortunato?" I rattled off through gritted teeth.

The knife descended toward my eyeball.

"He's dead!" I snapped out.

The knife stopped. Vito gave me a perplexed look. "No way."

"Yes, he is." The word must not have gotten out yet. I tried to calculate the hours since I'd left the little Greek café, but it didn't matter. "Him and his bodyguard."

"Bullshit," Vito said.

"True shit. Go make a few calls. Check it out."

He watched me carefully for a few moments, then shrugged. "Maybe I will. But say it's true. So the fuck what?"

"I'm the reason they're dead."

"Bullshit."

"True shit."

"You clipped the Italian Ninja? No way."

Obviously, what happened in Fucale's when I got the better of Fortunato never made it out to the masses. That was too bad, because it would've helped my credibility right about now. "He came there to clip me," I said. "It was self-defense."

"Well, good. You can tell that to the jury." He put a finger to his mouth. "Oh, wait. There ain't gonna be no fuckin' jury, is there? 'Cause you're finished, Bricks. This is fucking it. And you're full of shit, anyway."

"I'm not lying. You can find out. Make your calls. You'll see."

"Like I said, say it's true. So fucking what?"

I took a deep breath and let it out. "I gotta explain this to you?"

He slid the knife down my cheek. I don't think he drew blood, but when he poked the tip under my chin, I felt the bite and a drop well up under the blade. "Nah, we can skip all of this and get straight to the good stuff."

"Think about it. They want me whacked, so they send Fortunato? Why? He's a bodyguard, not a button man."

"Maybe he's got multiple talents. Why do I give a shit?"

"Because they picked him."

"So?"

"So they didn't pick you."

He gave me a confused look, lowering the knife. "What're you talking about?"

"Keeping a lid on this place might be what you're doing now," I explained, "but we both know it's not what you're best at. If they'd have sent you to clip me, would I be sitting here now? Or would you have gotten the job done right there at the diner, unlike Fortunato?"

He peered at me, confusion still clouding his gaze. "If I get sent to do a job, it gets done. But I still don't—"

"That's what I'm saying," I interrupted. "You're the

right man for the job, but they don't send you? You gotta wonder why. You gotta wonder if that means you don't factor into their long range plans, or maybe not even their short range ones. You gotta wonder—"

"I don't wonder jack shit," Vito protested. "Believe me."

"Why did they send Fortunato, then?"

"How the fuck am I supposed to know?"

I pushed forward. "More importantly, why didn't they send you?"

Vito just stared at me. "You're a crazy bitch," he muttered.

"Why, Vito?" I pressed. "Why didn't they send you to clip me?"

As I spoke, the door to the room swung open. Vito's eyes went to that direction, and mine followed. Max DaCosta stood in the doorway, his calm demeanor washing outward toward us both.

"I believe I can answer that question," DaCosta said, and closed the door behind him.

TWENTY-ONE
Cameron

Now I was pissed. And hurt. The stab wound wasn't as painful as I had feared. Maybe it was just endorphins or something, but it was more of a sore ache that burrowed deep into my gut than a sharp, searing pain. And it leaked only a little blood, considering.

Famous last words, right?

But now I was on the hunt and I couldn't stop to go to a hospital or anything. Whatever doubts I had about what I was doing had faded away. Fazzio had tried to kill me, twice now. Granted I came after him this last time, but I think it was my hesitation that kept me from doing the job.

Everything had happened so fast—my escape, meeting Vincent, finding Aunt Ruby and then seeking out Fazzio had been a blur. I was still so keyed up from surviving that blacked out room that I hadn't had much time to stop and think over what I was doing. I guess I treated it like a job. My new target was Fazzio and Son.

Oh, yeah, Pops—I'm coming for you too.

My waiting and wondering was over. I was a bulldog, a bloodhound. On the scent, out for a pound of flesh. I wasn't leaving this town until the threat against me had been neutralized. Chances were I'd be making new enemies who may likely come after me in the future. But for now, I wanted blood.

Tag and Boyd got me to their car and let me slump in

the back seat. They'd done okay for amateurs, but they were battered and more than a little freaked out by the killings.

When they dumped me, each stood up and surveyed their wounds.

"Fuckin' A," Tag said. Boyd nodded along. That about summed it up.

"Thanks," I said.

"I should be thanking you," Tag said. "That knife was coming for me if you hadn't stepped in there."

"I know my way around a gun. I thought it was better if I held it."

"Yeah, but." He pointed at my side and the dark stain of blood leaking down my shirt and into the top of my pants. "You got fucking stuck."

"Yeah, that sucked."

Boyd kept a hand pressed to his scalp. Blood ran down behind his ear, slicked down his hair in back and stained his collar. "We gotta get you to a hospital."

"I got one better."

I gave them directions to Vincent's. His wife was not happy about someone banging on the door at that late hour, but Vincent himself seemed pleased to see me again, and even more pleased that I needed more stitching.

"For this I can only close it," he said as he prepped a new needle and thread. "You really need to get a doctor in there to sew up the inside stuff."

"I know," I said. "And I will. But I got a few things to do first."

"Fazzio," he said.

"Yeah."

"You use the gun I gave you?"

I took his little pea shooter out of my pocket and handed it back to him, then drew Charlie's gun from my waistband and showed Vincent. "I found an upgrade."

Before Vincent stitched me again I had him look at Boyd's head. He said the boy would be fine without stitches, that head wounds just bleed a lot and look worse than they are. I got the sense Boyd didn't like hearing that. Made him seem like a pussy for making more of it than it was, and the way Vincent looked at him and Tag, pussies is probably exactly what he was thinking. To him, everything was better the way it was, including the men.

While Vincent went to work, in between grimaces of pain, I asked the boys a few questions.

"So where was the next stop if he hadn't been there? And is he likely to go there now?"

They shared a look. Tag said, "Saint Angelo Social Club."

Boyd added, "It's an old school place. Lots of deals get made there. You gotta be a member."

Vincent knew the joint. "Bobby Darin played there once. And Lou Monte. Now all they have is a jukebox. Nothing changes for the better, I tell you."

"So I couldn't get in?" I asked.

Tag chuckled, looked at the sorry state of me. "Uh, no. Not even on a good night."

"Hey, they're open for business, there's a way in," I said.

My two cousins shared a look filled with apprehension, and a little fear. I let them off the hook.

"You're not coming with me, boys."

They both exhaled, but didn't look necessarily calm yet. "You can't go in there by yourself," Tag said.

"That sounds like a dare." My bravado was undercut by my mewling whimper as Vincent dug the needle into my side again. "I just need to go look around and make a plan. It's a scout, and a one man team can make much easier work of that than three."

I eyed the gun on the counter next to Vincent and knew that if I had an opportunity, I would make the hit. But not without an exit strategy and not without knowing I had a clean shot on Fazzio that would put him down and end this for good. Since I started working with Bricks she'd taught me a lot about reducing risk in our work. Granted, I tended to be a bull in a china shop at times. But she taught me the value of good planning, good recon, good intel. She taught me not to let emotions rule the day. In this situation, that was hard. But I knew revenge could get your finger to pull a trigger, but it couldn't get you out of the room after it was done. Or out of the Saint Angelo Social Club in this case.

I thanked Vincent again and promised to take care of him financially when all this was over.

"No, no, no. You get rid of Fazzio and that's payment enough for me."

"But a man with your skills should be compensated," I said and I pointed at the rate sheet on the wall. It was yellowed and the prices seemed out of date by a decade, but they listed his services for hemming, altering, tailoring. Stitching knife wounds wasn't on the list, but we'd work out a fair deal.

I got the address to the club from Tag and Boyd and sent them on home to wait for me.

"If I'm not back by morning, I want you to find my partner, Bricks, down in the city. Ask around. She'll turn up. Tell her what happened. Tell her about Fazzio. She'll know what to do."

I felt like I'd just dictated my last will and testament.

"You sure, Cam?" Tag asked. "We could go with you and wait in the car."

"A car sitting idle with two mugs like you sitting doing nothing but watching the front of the club? They'd clock you faster than a whore spots an out-of-town businessman. No, I got this." I stuffed Charlie's gun back in my waistband and went outside to catch a cab.

The ride was short and my side ached with a dull heat. I mean it was actually warm if I held my hand over it. Chances were good I was doing more harm to myself and I'd probably end up dropping dead a minute after I got Fazzio, but revenge will make you do funny things.

When I stood up out of the cab, my knife wound screamed at me. My stitched-up arm didn't feel too hot either. Sitting still in the back of the cab let everything settle and now I was twisting my body to stand, rubbing the loose flaps of skin against each other, pulling wounds open when they just wanted me to shut up, sit still and let them heal.

The Saint Angelo was a tiny place with a red door it's only marking. A bouncer in a black suit jacket over a tight black T-shirt stood out front with one ass cheek on a stool. He watched the street, bored, and made a point of not looking at me when I got out of the cab a half block away.

I didn't even pass in front of the club. If there was any way in at all, the front door was last on the list. I found the alley running behind the club and ducked into it.

The alley smelled like the inside of my head felt. Rancid

and neglected. Finding the back door to the club was easy since they kept the red door motif. I was making my way past in as casual a manner as you can manage while sneaking through an alley, when an engine roar jerked my head up and away from the red door. There was a truck angling down the alley, the driver working hard not to scrape his fenders on the brick walls of the passway.

I pressed my body against a wall and watched him make tentative jerks forward until the cab of his truck was past the danger zone. The side of the truck came into view and it was a beer delivery vehicle. MASTRO'S DISTRIBUTION was printed on the side.

With a hiss of brakes the driver shut off the truck and the alley went quiet again except for the scurrying rats whose evening had been disturbed by the fat diesel engine. The driver pulled on a hat with his company logo and he was fighting with a jacket, complete with his name—JAMES—stitched over his heart. He couldn't get his arm through the right sleeve since it was twisted back in on itself. He seemed frazzled.

"Hey," I said.

"Not now, pal. I'm late as shit." He must have thought I was a bum looking for spare change. I was looking for something all right, and he had it. What he had was my opportunity.

He moved his clipboard to his mouth where he gripped it between his teeth so he could really work on that sleeve. That's when I clocked him with the butt of the gun. He grunted, spit out the clipboard, and fell forward. I hit him again on the way down.

He wasn't out, but he was stunned. Enough so that when he hit the scum-slick alley asphalt, he didn't put up a hand to protect himself. He hit with his chin first, teeth second and nose third. A triple play. He let out a long slow groan like he'd sprung a leak, and maybe he had.

I, on the other hand, make a sucking sound between my teeth. The swing of my arm threatened to undo all of Vincent's stitches in my side. I had to take a moment to hold my wound, make sure it wasn't bleeding again, and prep my body for more movement.

I also knew I had to work fast. I jerked his hat off first, put it on my head, then removed his jacket. The one arm was still empty which made it easier. I picked up the clipboard and went to knock on the red door.

Keeping my head down and trying to sound as Boston as I could, I shouted, "Delivery," and hoped this wasn't as bad of an idea as I thought.

TWENTY-TWO
Bricks

Max DaCosta approached me, walking in that measured but very efficient way of his. He was immaculately attired, as per usual, looking every bit the regal consigliere that he was. His gaze took me in, not smiling, not frowning, just impassive. I looked into his intelligent eyes, but they revealed nothing. Being a philosophy major, I'd always pegged DaCosta as a Marcus Aurelius fan. Nothing had changed since I saw him last to amend my opinion, although I thought he did look a little older. I guess that happens to us all, but I'd seen DaCosta less than a year ago. His appearance gave the impression it had been more like ten.

"Paula Brickey," he said. "I am surprised to see you."

"You don't look surprised."

A trace of a smile twitched on his lips. "I'm not, actually. More disappointed, I suppose. I thought you had better sense."

"I had better sense? What about you?"

He cocked his head slightly. "I'm afraid I don't understand what you mean."

I gaped at him. "You're fucking kidding me."

"I'm not, I assure you. Please explain yourself."

I glanced up toward Vito, then back to DaCosta. "Maybe your ape could put away his toy first? It's a little hard to talk with that thing hovering over me."

Vito bristled, but when DaCosta gave him a nod, he

stepped away, out of my line of sight. It was a small victory, but it felt good.

I tugged at the bindings on my wrists. "And these?"

He considered, then said, "Those remain in place for the time being."

"Come on. There's two of you, and I'm unarmed."

"Even so."

"It hurts," I said.

The twitch of a smile returned. "Paula, I am well aware of your many talents. Even wounded and outnumbered, you are dangerous."

A tiny, strange burst of pride went through me. I almost said thank you. How's that for deranged?

"One does not dare even the captive viper to strike, no matter the advantage," DaCosta continued. He considered me for another moment, then added, "Especially when one has not decided what to do with the viper he's captured."

"Technically, Vito Troglodyte over there caught me," I said. "But I see your point."

DaCosta found a chair and slid it across the floor to sit opposite me, stopping just outside of kicking range. He sat down, and crossed his legs European style. "So tell me, Paula. After everything that has happened, why did you come into a place that you knew was family owned?"

I could have answered him directly. I could have made this a thirty second conversation, but I needed time. Time to beat this situation. Whether I talked my way out or fought my way out, I need that time.

So I answered, "The pool hall isn't the only place I went."

"No?"

"No. I stopped by Albertini's barber shop earlier."

"Oh? I hadn't heard."

"You must be slipping."

He smiled indulgently. "Perhaps. But that establishment is no longer a business associated with the family."

"I figured that out. That's why I came to DeSasso's."

DaCosta's smile faded. "The RACKS 11 is under new ownership now."

I snorted sarcastically. The action made my head sing with pain. "Oh, believe me, I know."

"So my question remains. Why, after all this time, when there'd been no contact from the family, would you suddenly elect to march into a family owned establishment? To what end?"

I flexed the fingers in both of my hands. The feeling was nearly gone in them. DaCosta's gaze dropped to what I was doing, and he frowned slightly. He turned to Vito. "Has she been searched?"

Vito chuckled lasciviously. "Oh, yeah. I searched her real good. She ain't got nothing on her that God didn't put there."

"Then cut her free," DaCosta said. "But stand behind her."

I smiled at him. "Not so afraid of the viper now?"

He shrugged slightly. "A calculated risk, born of human kindness. I've always liked you, Paula. And your father. You know that."

Vito cut through my bindings roughly. I shook out my hands and rubbed my wrists to get the feeling to return. The blood rushed back into my hands immediately, and they exploded into painful prickles. Still, it was better than being tied up.

I felt, rather than saw, the looming presence of Vito

behind me. I tried to ignore him, focusing on DaCosta. "You keep talking about family, Max. Family establishment, the family, all of that. But what family do you mean? Not the Giordano family, that's for sure. You jumped ship from them."

DaCosta didn't react. He merely nodded slightly, and said, "A sinking ship, yes. I made a business decision, and it was clearly the correct one."

"Not very loyal, though, was it?"

"Loyalty, like all things, lies on a spectrum."

"How very relative of you. But kinda convenient."

DaCosta didn't reply right away. He simply watched me for a full minute, his implacable gaze seeming to invade my own thoughts. Going up against Vito, I'd been sure who was the smarter of us. Going up against DaCosta, it was a toss-up. Add to the fact I was in his place, with his goon standing behind me, eager to get busy with his knife, and it was clear: Advantage DaCosta.

But I was stalling like a motherfucker. There was that.

When he spoke again, he took away my only advantage. "Paula, let's not rehash old times. Let them lie. Instead, let's get to the heart of the matter. Why did you come to the pool hall today?"

"Why did you send Abe Fortunato to kill me?" I countered.

Genuine confusion flickered in his eyes. "Fortunato?"

"Don't act like you don't know his name," I said.

"I know who he is. But I haven't seen him since I changed positions."

"Changed positions? That's a clever euphemism, Max."

"It's an accurate statement. But let's stay focused, shall we? Why do you think I sent Fortunato?"

"Somebody did. And he used to work for you."

DaCosta brought his finger to his lips, thinking. "He attempted to assassinate you?"

"I think I said that."

"Why?"

I sighed. "Jesus, why does a guy like that try to clip anyone? Because someone sent him. Because you sent him."

"No," DaCosta said. "I assure you, I did not."

I hesitated. Max DaCosta had never lied to me, at least that I knew of. There were plenty of things he hadn't told me, but he'd never outright lied. And what would be the purpose of lying about it now, anyway? He had me at an extreme disadvantage. If he planned to kill me after this conversation, what purpose would lying hold at this point?

I switched gears slightly, running Vito's reaction through this new thought filter. It all added up the same.

"Have you worked it out?" DaCosta asked.

"I think so, yeah."

He spread his hands. "And your conclusion?"

"You're telling the truth. You didn't send him."

"Quite true."

"Then why this?" I motioned toward Vito and my surroundings.

DaCosta smiled thinly. "We had an uneasy truce, Paula, did we not? Your actions helped Don Trepani immensely in his takeover. There is considerable appreciation, and even some admiration, for what you accomplished."

"I wasn't alone," I said automatically, and immediately regretted it. The last thing I wanted to do was point these guys toward Cam.

"Even so," DaCosta continued. "You saved Don Trepani a great deal of work."

"But?"

He shrugged slightly. "However, regicide tends to make people uncomfortable."

"Only kings."

"Nervous king, nervous kingdom. So while I can assure you that Fortunato was not working for the Trepani family, I will also tell you that when the takeover was completed, there was initially some consideration that taking exactly such an action where you were concerned would be the best choice. After all, you killed a don."

"He deserved it."

"Perhaps we all do."

"Yeah," I said. "I saw that movie, too. Clint was great. What happened with Trepani? Why didn't he try to whack me?"

"I convinced him otherwise."

Of course. "How?"

"I assured him that you were smart, and that you were wise enough to avoid involvement in any family business ever again. I believe I even said that no one would ever see your face in these circles again." He gave me a mildly reproving look. "It appears I was wrong."

"Look," I said. "I wouldn't have come here if Fortunato hadn't moved on me. And you gotta admit, fingering you for that was the most logical conclusion."

"That is true," he admitted.

"And all I was doing here was looking for some answers. Trying to find a way to meet with you that was safe."

"It wasn't the greatest plan, Paula."

"No shit?" I touched my cheek where Vito had blasted me with the butt end of his knife. "So if you didn't send Fortunato, who did?"

"I have no idea."

"But you could find out?"

He looked at me, expressionless. Then a slow smile creased his lips. It might have been the most genuine smile I'd ever seen grace his face. "You have some balls, don't you, kid?"

The colloquialism seemed a little foreign coming from DaCosta, but all the same, it made Vito chuckle behind me. I made a mental note of his exact location. Whatever happened next, it was going to happen fast. And soon.

"What is it they say? Go big or go home?"

He nodded. "You clearly subscribe to that philosophy."

We'd gone from pre-murder banter to some kind of an understanding that maybe I'd walk away from this, to now me asking for information before I left. At least, that's where I'd been taking the conversation. I wondered if DaCosta had followed along, or if he was still back on step one.

He leaned forward, and motioned for me to do the same. When our heads were only a foot apart, he said, "I saved you once from Giordano. Do you remember?"

I nodded. I remembered it well.

"And then I saved you from Don Trepani, after you killed Giordano."

I didn't reply. What do you say to that? Thank you?

"And now here we are again, a third time. You've violated what is essentially a peace treaty by coming here. You've poked at the hornet's nest and stirred it up. You had the ill luck to come across a Taggliarti bent on family revenge. And your actions have brought me here to render a decision on your fate. Again." He leaned back, and turned his hands up to me. "What am I to do, Paula?"

I found my footing on the ground in front of me, and prepared to spring at him. But first, I gave him my best devil-may-care smile.

"You've done me a solid twice before," I said. "How about you go for the hat trick?"

TWENTY-THREE
Cameron

The door opened and I tilted my head down as if I was reading the clipboard. The bill of the company hat obscured my face.

"A little late," the guy said. I couldn't describe him because I didn't dare look at his face for fear he would see mine.

"Yeah," I said. "New route. I'll be quick."

"Whatever," he said and he walked away leaving the door open. Open. Just like that. These guys either had balls of steel to think they could handle anything that came in through that open door, or they were really fucking stupid. Mostly I think I was enjoying the benefit of a mid- to-low-level guy who thinks he's better than answering delivery doors in back. He wanted me to know how insignificant my job was by dismissing me.

I'd take it.

I went back to the truck and rolled up one of the side panels to reveal case after case of liquor and beer. I took the top case off the stack in front of me and winced in pain as my side protested the weight of the bottles. But this was my in. I needed to deliver something.

Walking through the back door let me in beside a long bar. The place was nearly empty and dimly lit. Music played as an afterthought. This was no dance club, it was a place where men wanted to be heard when they talked and even understood when whispering was called for.

I set the case of booze on the bar. Nobody there. In the shadows at the back of the bar I risked looking up and exposing my face. I saw a table near the front and at it Fazzio held court. He was too far away to hear, but there was a second bar on that far end. That bar top looked to be the main space. The lighting was better, the rail polished either by workers at night or by the elbows of regulars to the club.

I went back to the truck, grabbed another case and headed back. As I passed the driver where I'd stuffed him in a pile of trash and recyclable bottles, I heard him moan. Without setting down the case I kicked him in the head and he went silent again. Poor sap would probably have brain damage by the time this was through.

I carried my case of...I checked the side...Canadian Club to the front. I kept my head down and turned away from the table of men. As I got closer I could hear Fazzio's angry voice barking orders to his crew of six.

"Why can't I get a fuckin' answer on the broad?"

"It's all the way in New York."

"Yeah, it ain't fuckin' Mars. Get someone down there to call me, for fuck's sake."

"It's Trepani's territory now."

"Then call me a fucking Trepani!" Fazzio snapped.

That was a name I didn't want to hear. And the "broad?" I feared who they meant. I could hear though, and that was good. With my eyes down all my senses were rerouted to my ears. I listened more intently than I ever had before. I reached the bar and set down the case, consulted my clipboard like I was checking the list.

"Well, what about the two jerks?" Fazzio asked.

"It's coming."

"It ain't even breathing hard! Why can't I get some fuckin' answers?"

"You didn't give us much to go on, boss."

"I know I seen them before. And they gotta have some connection to Cameron."

One of the men stood and rushed out to make a phone call. Everyone ignored me.

What I needed now was an arsenal. An M-16 would cut a swath through all the guys facing me, but me with one handgun? Dead meat. I started to wish the cases contained grenades, not liquor. Maybe then I could take them out.

If I could figure a way to get Fazzio alone...Maybe the restroom? Fake that he has a phone call? Wait it out until he leaves for the night then ambush him?

The last one seemed the most likely candidate. I noticed one of the men looking my way, wondering, no doubt, why I'd been standing still so long. I tapped the clipboard as if I'd found the thing I was looking for and turned back to the rear door.

In the stink of the alley my thoughts jumbled together and failed to formulate a decent plan. I could go in blasting and hope for the best—never the right plan. I knew at least I couldn't hear too much info. Maybe once I knew their plans I could make one of my own. I lifted a third case of booze, this one a Johnnie Walker, and went back inside.

As I passed through the back door a man came jogging in the front. He went straight to Fazzio to deliver some news. I quickened my pace across the room to pick up the conversation.

"Got 'em," he said.

"Who are they?"

"Ruby Aldonatto's kids. Tag and Boyd."

Fazzio clapped his hands together once, a gunshot-loud cracking sound. "That's the fuckers. What stupid fuckin' names. Where are they?"

"I don't know where they are now, but I know where the Aunt lives. Best I could do for now."

I set the case of Johnnie Walker on the counter, my breath quick under my tilted hat.

The man went on, "Gimmie another hour or two and I'll get where they live."

"Fuck that," Fazzio said. "She'll tell us in two minutes if she's properly motivated."

I knew what that meant. So did his boys judging by the chuckles through the crowd. I wondered if each man there was hoping to get picked to do the motivating.

I really had to struggle not to pull my gun and shoot down Fazzio right there. I tried to figure what the chances were, without their leader, the gang of meatheads would lay down and not fight. Chances were slim.

"So let's go," one meathead said.

"Damn right," Fazzio said.

The same guy who'd been eyeballing me earlier stood and looked my way again.

"You need some help at your job there, pal?"

I must have jerked like when you wake up from a bad dream. I started to lift my head, but caught myself and kept it down at the clipboard. "All set," I said, trying my fake Boston accent out. "Forgot my pen." I patted my pocket a few times to show how my pen was missing, then I angled for the back door.

"Hey," he said. Some of the other men were looking my

way now, but I could tell the crowd wanted to move out and get to Aunt Ruby's house.

I stopped midway across the room. My gun weighed heavy in my waistband, ready for me to pull if I had to, but I really didn't want to. Not only was I outgunned, but these guys all wanted my blood and were willing to work through my family to get to me. If I made myself known now it would be like waking up in a pit of vipers.

"You can use mine," the guy said. I turned and looked out from under the visor of the hat. He held out a ballpoint pen. I walked slowly over to him while the other men, including Fazzio, stood and got ready to move out. Lucky for me, Fazzio was a stuck-up son of a bitch who didn't grace the help with his eye contact. He tried to ignore that a lowly delivery guy was even in the place.

I set the clipboard down, took the offered pen and made a few nonsensical marks on the form, then turned it for the guy to sign. He looked at it like it was written in Greek and scribbled an illegible series of peaks and valleys along the bottom of the sheet.

"Thanks," I said. I thought about saying something like *Go Sox* or *Yankees Suck*, but I figured that might be laying it on a bit thick. I just wanted to get the hell out of there and go warn Ruby and Tag and Boyd.

As I crossed to the back door I made a mental note for the next job—if there would be a next job—that a menial worker is a great disguise since nobody wants to deal with you or acknowledge that you're there. Maybe I could use that for a job someday. Man, I wished someday would come and I was back to killing for money and not revenge.

I closed the door behind me and took a deep breath of the foul air in the alley. Didn't matter what it smelled like right then, I made it out alive. The driver was making sounds again and moving so I hadn't caved his head in, which was good. I was going to steal his truck though.

After scraping off half the company logo in my less-than-skillful attempt to drive out of the narrow alley, I started out for Ruby's and hoped to hell I'd get there first.

TWENTY-FOUR
Bricks

Knowing you're going to die is a spiritual experience. It kicks yoga all to hell. Not that I'd recommend doing a getting-whacked sun salutation every morning, but facing the certainty of your own death has a particularly powerful impact on the soul.

I sat in that chair in the back room of RACKS 11, with Vito the slob impatiently twisting his knife just a couple of feet away, and watched DaCosta while he considered my fate. It was mostly for show, I was pretty sure. At any moment, he'd say something urbane, his suave voice tinged with regret, and that'd be the end.

Oh, I'd fight. I'd fight like a wildcat. And I'd get my first shot in at the old consigliere before turning to Vito and his blade. But Vito was big, he was strong, and he had a knife. For all I knew, he had a gun tucked in his waistband, too. And once DaCosta recovered from my initial blow, whatever weapon he had hidden away came into play. And the guy was resourceful. He once hit me with a Taser, though if I'm being honest, that was one of the two times saving my life that he mentioned earlier.

DaCosta stretched it out, his eyes boring into me while the gears behind them churned. I tried to keep my body loose but still coiled to spring when he gave Vito the word. These motherfuckers were not going to ice me and then go back to Trepani telling jokes about the experience, not if I had anything to say about it. Better that they were making excuses from the hospital, even if they did manage to finish the job.

I could feel the sweet rush of air as I drew it in and out of my lungs. I knew it had to reek of my sweat and Vito's breath in that room, not to mention whatever effete, old man cologne DaCosta wore, but I couldn't have told you so in that moment. To me, breathing was pretty fucking fantastic.

My ears were amped up, and I could hear Vito's breathing over my shoulder. I heard him shift from side to side. I could hear his lips smack while he waited. Hell, I might have been able to hear him blink.

All the while, my eyes met DaCosta's and I watched him think. Or pretend to think. For a moment or two, I tried to decide what I'd do in his place, but I pushed those thoughts away. It didn't matter. What mattered was what he did next. And more than that, what mattered was me exploding toward him.

My pops died in prison, fighting cancer. Even so, he kept his mouth shut, and he endured. It was a quiet death, but still a warrior's death. Now, I was going to die a warrior's death, too. I thought he'd be proud.

And with that, I was at peace.

Like I said, facing your own death kicks yoga all to hell.

DaCosta opened his mouth to speak. I tensed, barely hearing the words that came out of his mouth.

"All right, Paula," he said. "This last time."

I was already halfway out of my seat before the words registered. I forced myself to stop, and looked at him for confirmation. "Yeah?"

He nodded sagely. "I understand why you took the actions you took. And you haven't done anything to hurt the family's interests, so I can afford to be merciful here."

"Really?"

He nodded. "Really."

I glanced over my shoulder at Vito. His face housed an expression of surprise that was swiftly melting into rage. "Uh, Max..."

DaCosta followed my gaze. "Stand down, Vito," he said, his voice quiet but firm.

Vito jabbed a meaty finger toward me. "That bitch killed Bruno! You can't just give her a pass."

"Bruno is off the table," DaCosta said. "She already has a pass for that."

"Nuh-unh," Vito grunted, shaking his head. "She fucked that up when she came here."

I turned slowly so I was facing Vito, with DaCosta on my left. Things had changed so quickly, my head was reeling. I found myself hoping DaCosta was carrying a rocket launcher or something under that jacket, but I didn't see any tell-tale lumps.

"That," DaCosta told Vito, "is not your decision."

Vito hesitated, then snarled back, "Whattayou think the boss will say about your decision? I don't think he'll be too happy he has some kind of pussy working for him."

DaCosta reached into his pocket. Everyone tensed. His hand came out with a cell phone. "Let's call him and see. We can inquire about my decision-making discretion first, and then we'll ask him how he views insubordination and soldiers with their own personal agendas. How about that?"

Vito squinted a little, like he had trouble understanding what DaCosta said. The proffered phone had to be a clear enough message for him, though.

Just in case it wasn't, I chimed in. "He's saying you can go ahead and call Dad, but all Dad's going to say is that he's right and you're getting grounded for being an asshole."

Vito's gaze snapped to me. His face purpled and contorted with fury. "You murdering whore!" He took a step toward me, extending the knife.

DaCosta stepped calmly between us. "Enough, Vito," he said smoothly.

Vito didn't hesitate. He drove the blade of his knife straight into DaCosta's chest, right up to the hilt. DaCosta let out a soft gasp. Vito's crazy leer darkened with greater intensity. He withdrew the knife slowly, and DaCosta crumpled almost soundlessly to the floor.

"Now you," Vito growled.

He lunged toward me. I recoiled, just out of range. He lumbered forward and swung wildly at me. I ducked, feeling the rush of air as his hand and the knife passed above my head. He reversed direction immediately, coming at me with a backhand stroke. I side-stepped and brought both hands up to deflect. My left ended up catching him at the elbow and my right naturally found his wrist. I didn't have time to grab anything, though. Vito pulled his arm straight back, then lunged and slashed at my mid-section.

I felt the cool snick of the blade, followed by warmth.

Fuck!

I moved to the side, circling away from his knife hand. Vito stalked me aggressively, and I didn't dare look down to see how bad the cut on my stomach was. My knees hadn't given out yet, which I took as a good sign. If my insides were hanging over my belt, I was pretty sure I would have run out of steam.

Then again, maybe I was running on nothing but adrenaline.

Vito slashed again. I dodged and circled. The room was small, and I moved to put the chair he'd tied me to between us. It was bolted to the floor, so he'd have to go around it.

Or so I thought.

The resourceful fucker tracked me until the chair back wasn't between us any more, then he leapt up onto the chair and dropped in front of me. He landed with a grunt, but didn't hesitate. He drove his knife toward my face.

I shifted to my right to avoid the thrust, lowered my shoulder and powered forward like an offensive lineman. The point of my shoulder struck him right in the solar plexus. His breath whooshed out over the top of me.

Before he could recover, I gave him a hard shot to the balls as I slid around his body to the back side. He stood frozen for a second, then started to move again. I leapt onto his back, wrapping my arms around his throat and sinking my heels into his thighs.

He still hadn't caught his breath from the shoulder I drove into him, and now I had his breath cut off. I adjusted my grip and went for the carotid artery to put him to sleep. His thick neck made it difficult, but I got the hold and clamped down.

I immediately knew I had it right, because Vito started to flail in panic. I heard the knife clatter to the floor and felt his meaty fingers clawing at my arms. I dipped my chin and buried my face into his shoulder and squeezed for all I was worth.

A few glancing blows rang off the top of my head, right where Fortunato's punch had landed in what seemed like a lifetime ago. Vito twisted from side to side, as if he were considering throwing me off like I was some kind of a bronco rider, but he couldn't generate any force.

If he'd been smart, he'd have slammed backward into a wall. That would have given him a chance. But Vito wasn't smart. I'd been right enough about that.

It took longer than eight seconds, but slowly Vito sank to his knees. Finally his hands dropped listlessly to his sides and we both toppled sideways to the floor. He took most of the brunt of the landing, and I managed to keep my grip on this neck. I maintained the hold for another fifteen seconds before releasing it. I knew that once I let it up, he'd be awake again within thirty seconds. Maybe sooner.

I rose from the floor and checked Vito's beltline. Nothing. Then I noticed he was wearing a shoulder rig under his track suit. A major fashion faux pas, but I was happy for it. I grabbed the pistol and jerked it from the holster. It was a Smith & Wesson, and given Vito's personality, I couldn't imagine it was a small caliber. The heft in my hand felt good.

When I turned to DaCosta, I could see he was still breathing. A small puddle of blood had already pooled beneath him. His eyes were open but unfocused. That wasn't good.

I looked around the room and spotted my purse on the floor next to a filing cabinet in the corner. I grabbed it and pulled out my cell phone. While I kept Vito's still form covered with his own pistol, I dialed 9-1-1.

"Nine, one, one. Please state your emergency."

"RACKS 11, used to be RACK 'EM UP pool hall. It looks like Vito Taggliarti just stabbed Max DaCosta in the back room. He's bleeding badly, so send help fast."

"Ma'am, I need some information from you—"

I hung up.

Vito stirred slightly, letting out a light moan. I stepped over and kicked him in the head as hard as I could. He fell still again.

Jesus, that felt good.

I squatted down next to DaCosta. He blinked up at me this time. His expression was cloudy, but I could tell he was conscious now. I took first one hand, then the other and put them over his wound.

"Press hard, Max. The cops are coming, and so are the medics."

"You..." His voice rattled weakly in his throat.

"I can't stay," I said. I pressed down on his hands again. "Keep the pressure on. It won't be long, all right?"

He might have nodded at me. I couldn't tell, and if he did, the movement was too slight to be sure. I didn't have time to wait for anything more. I stood, kicked Vito once more in the back of the head, and went to the door.

That's when I remembered the guard. Why he hadn't come in during the fight was beyond me, unless he'd been told to stay out no matter what. It didn't matter. He was one more obstacle I had to get through to get the hell out of this place.

I leveled the gun with my right and flung open the door with my left.

TWENTY-FIVE
Cameron

I realized pretty quick that I'd left the roll door open on the side of the truck. Cases of liquor dumped out onto the street and surely made some wino very happy. The bottles that didn't break, anyway.

I'd paid pretty good attention in the cab on the way there that I was able to retrace the route back to Aunt Ruby's fairly easy. A habit since I was a kid. I was always watching road signs, street names. I like knowing where I am. With my life lately, you'd never know it.

Probably because I was moving alone and not in the wagon train of cars Fazzio and his boys were in, I made good time and rolled up on Aunt Ruby's house before them. It didn't hurt that I couldn't have cared less about the truck and I made a few questionable yellow lights and scraped the paint off a few parked cars on the way. When I parked the delivery truck on the street I left the keys in it and didn't look back. If they had the balls to take it, some kids from BU were gonna have party supplies for a month.

I left the hat and clipboard and took Charlie's gun with me. When I knocked on the door, Tag answered.

"They're coming," I said as I pushed past him.

"Who is?"

"Fazzio. And he's not alone."

"Shit."

Boyd showed up and Tag filled him in. The two of them spun in circles like confused dogs for a while. An unexpected turn like this really threw them for a loop. Then Aunt Ruby showed up.

"What's going on?"

I explained. "Fazzio recognized Tag and Boyd. He and his guys are on their way here now. We gotta get you out."

"Fazzio's coming here?"

"Yeah. Grab your purse and let's go."

She clapped her hands once in front of her, made one of those Italian hand gestures that means bastard or sends out a curse or something. "Fuck him. Let him come."

She went to the hall closet. Tag and Boyd were still scared and, from what I could tell, on the verge of holding each other for comfort.

"He's got a bunch of guys with him, Aunt Ruby. We can't stay."

"The hell I can't," she said. "This is my house for fifty years. No piss-ant needle-dick is gonna run me off." She bent into the closet and when she stood back up she held a double barreled shotgun. She needed two hands to hold it and in her tiny arms it looked like she's taken the anti-aircraft gun off a battleship.

"Nobody's gettin' in here without an ass full of lead."

I didn't know what to say. I knew Tag and Boyd wanted to leave. As much as I wanted to take out Fazzio and any of his crew that wanted to die with him, we were outnumbered and it didn't look like a fair fight.

"Aunt Ruby, I really think we should go."

"I know what you do," she said, staring through me with eyes as black as those double barrels.

"What do you mean?"

"I know your job for the family. Button man, right?"

There was no use lying to her. I at least tried to hedge it. "I've killed people before."

"So do it again." Ruby stood steadfast before me. She was as unmoving and resolute as General Patton. It was impressive to see and more than that, she made anyone who didn't match her courage feel like a pussy.

I'd checked Charlie's gun and found six shots. Not a lot. I'd have to make every one count. I was sure Tag and Boyd would need something stronger than hockey sticks.

"What about them?"

Ruby leaned the shotgun against the door frame of the closet and ducked back inside. She came out with two Magnum .45s. Big ass guns which she handed to my two cousins. They looked at the heavy metal in their hands like she'd given them nuclear warheads.

By the time I turned around to her she handed me another gun. A .44 Magnum. The Dirty Harry gun. I'd never even held one. Why Aunt Ruby had this arsenal in her closet I didn't want to know, but I was grateful for it. However, even with this kind of firepower in my hand and understanding the slight advantage we had in knowing they were coming, I still felt the best bet was to get out and live to fight another day.

"Aunt Ruby, I—"

Too late. Outside, tires screeched on the pavement. They weren't trying to hide their arrival. I peered out the decorative window set into the front door and saw three cars all emptying out, four men to a vehicle. Twelve against four. Well, here went nothing.

I pointed at Tag and Boyd. "Behind the couch. Use it as cover but don't let anyone get through the door. If we can bottleneck them we can pick 'em off one by one." I put a hand on Ruby's shoulder and positioned her around the half wall in front of the stairs.

"You sure you can use that thing?" I asked her.

"Just you watch." The pockets of her cardigan rattled with extra shells.

"Where's the back door?"

"That way." She pointed through the kitchen to a small mud room with a washer and dryer. I ran that way, stuffed the .44 in my waistband next to Charlie's now outclassed 9 mm. I pulled the dryer away from the wall and shoved it in front of the back door, then yanked the washer away and planned to make a double stack of obstacles when Ruby's first shotgun blast rang out.

I left the washer halfway out and figured the dryer would have to do. It'd slow them down anyway.

The front entry was a mess already. Splintered wood and falling plaster from Ruby's first blast still hung in the air and now pops of gunfire lit up the front door from outside. I saw blood on the doorframe and I knew Ruby had gotten at least one of them, probably whoever the sucker was who got voted first through the door. He didn't make it. So down to eleven now.

Tag and Boyd cowered behind the sofa as the barrage of gunfire continued. Most of the bullets stuck in the walls of the solidly built house. The siding on the outside was over brick like most of the houses in Boston. Handguns didn't stand a chance. They'd have to try the door again.

I back-stepped up the stairs until midway. I was out of the line of fire but had a good top down view of the front entryway. The shooting slowed, then a powerful foot kicked in the door and finished the job the shotgun started.

Ruby let loose again with barrel number two and a dead body fell inside through the gaping door.

"Go to hell, you sonofabitch!" Ruby said.

Ten to go. Tag and Boyd both raised up together like they'd been planning and counting down behind their barricade. They each fired two shots at the general vicinity of the door and then ducked down again. Nobody was hit.

I heard the back door kick in and slam into the dryer blocking the way. I moved quickly down the steps and when I reached the bottom I saw a dark figure fill the door. I fired and holy shit the kickback from the .44 nearly made me drop it. I swear it was louder than the shotgun, too. Got the bastard though. Nine left.

I also tweaked my side and the sharp daggers of pain were back. A stitch had torn free or something like it. Each step was a new spike of pain, but I didn't stop as I turned and headed back through the kitchen. I raised the Magnum and fired three shots at the sitting ducks trying to wedge the door open against the dryer, which was itself wedged against a tall cabinet. That door wasn't going anywhere.

Wood fragmented, blood spurted, men grunted and we were four to six. No Fazzio yet.

Ruby had reloaded. She sent another cannon blast at the hole where the former front door lived. Most of that shot carried outside and probably made it as far as the neighbor's house across the street. In houses up and down the block, 9-1-1 calls were being made. I knew that for certain.

I leaned back against the fridge in a sudden, urgent need

to take a break. My side ached like the knife was back in it. I saw more movement outside the back door and I fired again with the Magnum. No hit, but the recoil on that gun was hell on my knife wound.

I dropped the Harry Callahan special on the counter and drew the smaller weapon I'd borrowed from Charlie.

A new volley of gunfire from the front room drew my attention back there. Chances were slim anyone would be getting through the back door at all, so I went back out to help.

Tag and Boyd were up and firing. Two men were trying to slither through the opening, staying low and using the dead men as cover. A shot caught Boyd in the shoulder and he went down behind the couch again. Tag kept shooting and popped the guy who shot his brother in the crown of his head. The pile of wreckage in the doorway was spattered in blood.

Ruby had been keeping herself covered around the half wall. She rotated her body out, let loose a banshee scream and leveled that shotgun at the other man now wiping bits of his pal out of his eyes. He never saw the blast coming. His hands up around his eyes were cut off at the wrists. The blast took out most of his neck too.

A shot came out of the darkness on the front lawn and hit Ruby in the chest. She took two staggering steps back and hit the bottom stair, fell down on her backside with her arms as wide open as her mouth. She looked like she wanted to give a hug to whoever came through the door next. But what came through next was another bullet. Her body shook and she fell back onto the stairs. She lay there, sprawled over the bottom five steps of her beloved house and I watched her die.

I lost track of the math, but seeing Ruby dead and the shotgun neutralized seemed to embolden Fazzio's remaining crew. They stormed the gates.

All I kept thinking was—this place is a fucking slaughterhouse. This is my element.

First guy in the door caught my bullet in his knee. He went down, clearing a path to the guy behind him who I hit in the chest. They each got off a wild shot that hit the ceiling and never posed a threat.

I heard a voice outside, "Go, just go." Fazzio.

I stepped forward, knowing he was going to get away. Even in the midst of this mayhem, he was calling for his driver. I stepped past Aunt Ruby and moved toward the door. The guy I'd given a knee shot to moved and raised his gun at me. In the corner of my eye I saw the movement, but I was too late to do anything about it.

Tag fired from his sofa foxhole. The man fell dead on top of his partner. I gave a quick look over my shoulder and nodded a thanks at Tag who was already bending down to help his brother.

I leapt through the open hole of a door and when I came down on the front porch, my side screamed in protest. I could feel fresh, warm blood running down my side. I saw Fazzio closing the back door on one of the three cars, another man in the driver's seat frantically clawing at a set of keys. This hadn't gone the way they expected.

I kinda wished for the .44 back.

With lights popping on all up and down the block, I raised my gun and shot the driver twice. The engine hadn't even started.

It was harder to lift the gun now with my side aching

the way it was. Harder to walk too, but I pushed on through the wet grass. I wondered if it was nighttime dew or blood I was slipping on. Fazzio looked trapped in the backseat—a caged animal. He seemed to be scrambling in his waistband for a gun. Who knows how long since he'd had to use one. Either way, it wouldn't be tonight. I got close enough to the side of the car so I knew I wouldn't miss and used my last two shots on the man who'd lured me up to Boston and imprisoned me.

I wasn't getting paid for this hit, but I relished the sight of blood spraying the inside window and getting caught in little rivulets of the cracked glass surrounding the bullet holes. As I watched Fazzio's blood slide down the glass, I felt my own blood soak into my pants.

The adrenaline crash let the pain through the door and my legs buckled. My knees hit the wet lawn and I heard sirens. I had to get away, but there was no way I was getting very far in my state. I began to crawl on hands and knees. I felt pathetic as I moved like a dog looking for a place to lift his leg, but my body wasn't about to let me stand any more. I'd abused the stamina and brief energy rush to do further damage to myself.

I wanted to go tell Tag to run, take Boyd with him, but I had to assume they weren't so dumb as to hang around and talk to cops when they got there. For me, I was headed for the neighbor's yard. Their lights hadn't gone on so either they were too scared or they were out for the night.

I hit the dry concrete of the driveway separating the two properties and kept up my crawl. Then I hit my first obstacle—a chain link fence. I pulled at the bottom like we used to do as kids when places like construction sites wanted to keep us out, but we wanted to see what they hell they were protecting. It worked like when I was ten, but I wasn't the same skinny kid as back them. I didn't slide under quite so well. Pushing and pulling myself along on my back, the bottom edge of the chain link cut my torso, tore my shirt and dug scrapes into my face as I pulled the last of my body through.

I started to think the neighbors were out of town when I saw the dog run but didn't see or hear a dog. That's all I needed right then was to have some watchdog set upon me smelling like raw meat and fear. Making it into the house was too much, but I had the next best thing. As I heard the sirens pull onto the block, I tucked myself into the dog house and passed out.

TWENTY-SIX
Bricks

The guard's eyes were as big as boiled eggs when I thrust the gun in his face.

"Your pistola," I told him. "Now."

He swallowed and reached for it.

"No," I said. "Left hand."

He stopped, then used his left hand to unsnap the holster.

"Two fingers," I said.

He levered the gun out with his thumb and index finger and held it out to me. I snatched it and dropped it unceremoniously into my purse. "Nice job, Guido. Now we're going to play a little game called Paramedic. You get your ass into that room, and you use your palms to put direct pressure on Max's gut. You get me?"

He gave me a confused look. "His...?"

"Just get in there and keep pressing down on his stomach until the medics get here. Understand? You'll be a fucking hero." I stepped around him carefully, then waved him inside the room with the barrel of Vito's gun. "Hurry up."

His expression was still confused, but he turned and headed into the back room anyway.

"Hey!" I called after him.

He stopped and looked over his shoulder at me.

"Direct pressure. Just hold it," I said. "Don't pump. It's not CPR, huh?"

He nodded, and made for DaCosta's fallen form on the floor.

I turned away and headed down the hall, lowering the pistol to my side. I tried to walk fast but not too fast to draw attention. I knew there still some guys I might have to deal with in the main business area. At least two guidos playing pool, and probably the dope slingers further away, too. Maybe the bartender, though I doubted he'd get involved.

Of course, that's if DaCosta didn't bring any muscle along with him. I could be walking into a battalion of guys in silk suits, tracks suits, or both.

I slowed down near the end of the short hallway. The door in front of me had to lead into the main room. Off to the side were two other doors. I peered into one. It was a storeroom with no other exits. The other room was a bathroom.

With a window.

I stared at the window for a few seconds, doing a little math in my head

Close, I thought. It would be close.

I stepped into the bathroom, locked the knob and slid the privacy lock. It probably wouldn't slow anyone down, but I wanted every advantage I could get.

I dropped Vito's gun into the sink where I could grab it again if someone came crashing in, and I turned to the window. When I closed the toilet lid and stepped up onto it, I felt the first sting of pain in my stomach. I examined the cut quickly, lifting my slashed shirt and looking at my belly. The wound had almost stopped bleeding, with just a slow ooze still pushing out from the folds of skin. I probed at it delicately. The skin around the cut barely gave way.

I was lucky. As knife wounds go, this one was pretty superficial.

I had to lean perilously on the toilet seat to get to the window latch. My mind flashed insanely to Cam's toilet dance when he garroted the German, and I almost smiled.

Focus!

I reached for the window lock. When I got it unlatched, I was too stretched out to have any leverage to push it open. So I slung my purse over my shoulders crosswise, Indiana Jones-style, climbed up on the toilet tank and jumped for the window ledge.

My right hand grabbed on, but my left slipped off the ledge. I scrambled with my feet along the wall, making noises like a scurrying rat, and whipped my elbow up onto the ledge. Then I pushed the window open, clambered up on the ledge, and squeezed through. It was tight, and I knew I was leaving streaks of blood behind me.

I half-controlled my descent into the alley way, slowing my fall with one hand on the outside of the ledge, but unable to hold on enough to stop it. The muscles in my chest were singing with the effort, and I could feel new wetness at my midsection.

Later, I thought. Deal with it later.

I walked the hell out of there.

Two blocks away, I bought a black sweatshirt from a street vendor and pulled it over my head. That covered up most of the blood so people wouldn't notice me. It was amazing how comforting it was to sink back into that thriving anonymity that is this city.

The bleeding had stopped. In a public restroom, I made

sure, examining the cut again, this time with more patience. I was surprised at how shallow it was. It wasn't exactly a paper cut, but it didn't look nearly as bad as I thought it would. I guess it's true what they say. Life is a game of inches.

My apartment was still out of the question, so I found a coffee shop and sat in a corner booth, my back to the wall. Surprisingly, I was starving, so I scarfed down a sandwich and some fries. I did so without thinking, letting my mind settle after everything that had happened. When I was full, I ordered a second cup of coffee, leaned back and thought things through.

I believed DaCosta. He hadn't sent Fortunato. And while there were still people out there like Vito who might want me dead, I don't believe anyone in Trepani's crew would defy him enough to seek me out. Besides, someone like Vito would just walk up behind me at my apartment door or catch me on the street or something straightforward like that. Setting up a meet like they did wasn't a bush league move. It was something a little more strategic, and strategic meant some kind of boss.

But who?

I had no fucking idea.

I sat and thought and drank down that second cup of coffee, then switched to water.

Still no clue.

Finally, I realized it didn't matter. This city was gone for me, as much as I loved it. I couldn't live here as prey, and even if I figured out who started this and dealt with him, I was persona non grata with Trepani's family now, too. I needed an exit strategy.

But first, I had to find Cam.

* * *

After I tried his cell phone again and got no answer, I smashed my phone and threw it in the trash. I wasn't sure they'd be able to identify my number from the 9-1-1 call, but my guess was they had that technology available to them. So the cops probably already knew I was the one who called in the mess at RACKS 11, which was one more reason to leave this city behind.

I realized then that I didn't even know if Cam was here in the city or still in Boston.

So how the hell was I supposed to find him?

In the end, the answer was easy. So easy, I should have thought of it before, but I suppose I was too caught up in my own mess to think clearly.

Tia.

I hopped on the subway and headed for the house Cam shared with her.

Tia never liked me, not one bit. She couldn't seem to decide if I was competition for Cam's romantic attention, or if I was the best friend who led him astray and got him into shit. So instead of deciding one way or the other, I got the double whammy of jealous girlfriend hatred from her on both fronts. Needless to say, I hadn't been to their home more than a couple of times.

I stopped at a pharmacy near the subway stop and bought a few first aid supplies. When I knocked on the front door of their place, I had an absurd hopeful moment that Cam would answer the door. But it was Tia, and she wasn't glad to see me.

Imagine that.

"He's not here," she said abruptly.

"I know," I said. "Can I come inside? I need to talk to you."

She looked me up and down, saving most of her disdain for the tourist bait sweatshirt I was still wearing. Then she said, "Why can't we talk here? I can hear you just fine."

"I need to use the bathroom."

Her lip curled a little, but then she sighed and stepped aside to let me in. "It's down the hall."

I knew where it was. I spent about ten minutes rinsing off my cut, then applying anti-bacterial cream, and finally some gauze bandaging. I started to tape some gauze over the cut, then changed my mind and just wrapped an entire package worth around my mid-section. I figured that would hold it in place better anyway.

When I came out, I found Tia in the kitchen with a cup of coffee. She looked up, but didn't offer me any. That was fine. I'd had my fill of coffee before I got on the subway, and I'd had my fill of her about thirty seconds after the first time we met.

"You were in there, like, forever," she said, wrinkling her nose. "You sick?"

I shook my head. Instead, I raised my shirt to show her the bandage. "Just injured."

She shrugged. "You slither with snakes, sometimes you get bit."

"True enough," I agreed. "But I'm more worried about Cam right now. Has he called?"

I expected a little concern from her, but I should have known better. What I got was that same schizophrenic jealousy flashing in her eyes. "I figure you'd know better than me. You're his partner, right?"

"Tia..."

"Why should I tell you, anyway?"

"Because he might be in danger. And I can help him."

She considered, but her expression didn't soften much, if at all. "He called," she said finally.

"Is he all right?"

"He said he was. But he sounded a little funny."

"Funny how?"

"Like a clown," she snapped. "What do you think? He sounded like he wasn't completely all right. Plus he said things went a little sideways."

I bet they did, I thought. Sideways with a bullet.

"Do you have any idea where he is right now?"

"I'm not sure. But he said he was going to his Aunt Ruby's."

"Where's that?"

"Boston." She sipped her coffee and frowned at me.

I suppressed a sigh. "Do you know her last name?"

"Aldonatto."

"An address?"

Tia glared at me. "Why don't you check a phone book when you get there?"

I stood up. "It's been a pleasure, Tia."

As I walked toward the door, toting my pharmacy bag of medical supplies, I heard her slide the chair back from the kitchen table. I braced myself for the tirade I expected was coming, but it never came. At the front door, I glanced back at her. She stood in the kitchen doorway, arms crossed, a curious mixture of snotty anger and creeping concern on her face.

"Do me a favor," she said, her tone bitter.

I paused, my hand on the door knob. "What's that?"

She didn't answer right away. I waited for what seemed like a full minute before I decided she wasn't going to say anything after all. But when I turned the knob and pulled open the door, she finally spoke.

"Take care of him," she said hoarsely.

I didn't answer. I just left.

I was lucky to catch the last train that night to Boston. I sat in a car with three other passengers. We spread out and did a good job ignoring each other. I dozed a little bit, but I was still edgy from everything that had happened, so I started awake every so often, glancing around the near empty car, looking for Vito or some other Trepani soldier.

The problem now was that in addition to making myself a target for Trepani, I still had no idea who was behind the attack on me and whatever went "sideways" with Cam. I hoped he knew, but until I found him and we got caught up, pretty much anybody could be one of "them" sent to clip me.

Jesus, I thought. Listen to me. I sound like a paranoid meth freak.

No one entered or left the train car for the entire trip. I could hear some light snoring coming from one of my traveling companions, and the occasional rustle of movement from the other two, but it was all benign. Nothing to be paranoid about.

Even so, I barely slept all the way to Beantown.

***

It was early morning by the time I arrived at the MBTA station. I caught a cab outside the station, and asked the cabbie if there were any libraries that were open twenty-four hours. He looked at me funny, and I couldn't tell if he thought I was crazy or if he didn't know what a library was.

I switched gears and asked him to take me to a FedEx store, and when he pulled up in front of it, I was relieved to see the OPEN sign burning in the window. That's one thing you can always count on in this world: commerce.

The FedEx store had a rack of reference material next to the cashier. I found what I was looking for on the top shelf. Most of the world might be digital, but for some reason we were still killing trees to print the phone book. I thumbed through it while a twenty-something clerk with greasy hair and greasier skin watched me suspiciously.

Aldonatto was a more common name than I thought it'd be, but it didn't take Sam Spade to figure out that ALDONATTO, A. & R. was my best bet. I tore out the sheet of paper, and replaced the book on the shelf.

"Hey!" the clerk said. "You can't do that!"

"I just did," I told him. "Call the cops."

"Selfish bitch!" He yelled at me as I went out the door.

I walked a block and a half before I was able to catch another cab. I gave him Aunt Ruby's address and sat back in the seat to watch the cityscape of Boston flit by.

The place was a war zone. Several cars were parked at haphazard angles in the street. One had an explosion of darkening blood inside it. The cops had strung crime scene tape around the area in a half-assed attempt to keep people back, but it was only partially working. Even in the creeping light of morning, there had to be thirty or forty people milling around, watching everything the cops were doing. A single television news van was parked as close as it could to the scene, its satellite transmitter extended high in the air. A perfectly coiffed news reporter stood nearby with a camera man, checking her makeup in the van's side mirror.

Even from a distance, I could see the house was shot all to hell. Several bodies blocked the entry way. It was impossible to be sure from the angle I had, but there had to be at least three bodies stacked up where the front door used to be. Maybe more. I glanced at the numbers on the house, though I didn't need to. This had to be Aunt Ruby's. Cam's fingerprints were all over this mess.

I walked slowly around the assembled crowd, checking out the view from all the vantage points I could. It was difficult to get a good look at the bodies, and I couldn't tell if any of them was Cam or not. A couple had the wrong body type, but with others, it was hard to tell. I wondered why the cops hadn't moved them yet, but I guess they figured dead was dead, and they left them in place to investigate the scene.

"What happened?" I asked one old lady on the fringe of the crowd, but she just scowled at me like I had asked her if she wanted me to rub some shit on her face, so I moved away. A few minutes later, I nudged a guy who looked like a plumber. "What happened?" I repeated.

He just shrugged. "Some guys decided to shoot up the Aldonatto place, I guess."

"Who?"

He shrugged again. "Fazzio, I heard." He pointed to the

car with the blood spatter all over the inside. "That's him, I'm pretty sure."

I got the feeling I was supposed to know who Fazzio was, but I didn't. I resisted the urge to ask about him. Instead, I asked, "Why?"

He gave me another shrug. "The fuck I'm supposed to know? You ask me, though, I figure it was one of Ruby's boys. Tag and Boyd, the fucking retards."

I nodded like I knew who that was. "What about Ruby?"

This time he didn't shrug. He spat on the ground instead. "Fuckers shot the old lady in her own house. You believe that? What's this world coming to? Used to be people had respect, even people like Fazzio. Hell, especially people like him. Now? They just blast a sweet old lady who never did nothing to nobody."

I nodded, then slipped away. I got all I was going to get out of him, and I didn't want to be remembered.

I wandered around the fringe of the crowd, looking at the assembled group to see if maybe Cam was there, pretending to be a bystander. I listened to snatches of conversation but didn't hear any references to my partner. I spent about an hour working my way around the gaggle, until I finally ended up standing in one of the neighbor's yard near an empty dog run. I watched the cops work at the speed of molasses, and I watched the sun come up and peek through the row houses.

I had absolutely no idea what to do next.

TWENTY-SEVEN
Cameron

I'd seen a lot of things since I climbed into that dog house—mostly blackness. In and out of consciousness, woken by police chatter, sirens, cops and bystanders reacting to the carnage. Listening to it all play out like a radio show made me realize people only had about three reactions to violence like that: "Holy shit!" "What the fuck?" and "Oh my God." I'd heard all three of those on a loop every time anyone new showed up.

Now I had my strangest vision yet. My world had been going a little dark at the edges for a few hours. The tiny dog house door I could see through on the rare occasion my eyes were open didn't help. My vision began to warp and dim. The cops were as much a product of the flashing lights as any human forms. It was like I'd taken mushrooms or something, but was really only blood loss.

Then I saw her: my mother. My first thought was, great, she's here to say I told you so. I'd killed Uncle Rocco and now I'd gotten Aunt Ruby shot. It would please my mom to no end to see me curled up in a dog house slowly dying while help was only half a front lawn away, but I couldn't make a sound because between dying in a dog house and spending the rest of my life in prison—well, scratch my ears and feed me a milk bone. I'm dying right here. All dogs go to heaven, right?

But my mother didn't talk to me. She seemed more interested in the cops and the circus that was winding down in Ruby's front yard. The lights had stopped flashing after they realized there was no one to save. The news van peeled out and rushed away to make the deadline for the news at eleven. Neighbors drifted back home and really only wanted to know the answer to one question: would there be more of this?

Mom stood with her back to me, not even noticing the smell of her own son's blood. The dog smells probably covered it up.

My limbs were stiff from being in the fetal position for so long. I really wished this family had gone with a larger dog. I was cold, but sweating. I could feel blood coagulating on my clothes and my skin. At first my wounds bled warmth, now they chilled my bones.

Then I thought to myself—why the fuck would my mom be here? She wouldn't. But I knew that woman. I'd swear it.

It was the shoes. The sensible, all purpose, fashionless and worn out shoes on her feet, which were eye level with me. She found me. Bricks.

Holy shit. What the fuck? Oh my God.

Things got fuzzy for a while. I know I tried to say her name, but it came out as a mumbled groan. Her face came into focus. She kept it together. Didn't say a word and urged me to do the same. There were still cops, still onlookers, but their attention was next door.

I wanted to explain about my knife wound, but it would have been too much and been sounds we didn't need to make. Besides, as soon as she birthed me out of the dog house she saw for herself. I was a newborn cow, all slick with blood and other mess, unable to stand, confused looking and wide-eyed.

Bricks dragged me to the back yard of the neighbors. She laid me out and I could stretch my arms and legs, which didn't happen without protest from my muscles. I managed not to scream. She whispered a lot of questions and I whispered back half answers and nonsense. I could tell she was getting frustrated and I wasn't being much help.

I decided to ask her a question. "How'd you find me?"

"Tia."

I nodded and forced a smile.

"How do we get out of here?" she asked.

The way these row houses were laid out the long driveways ran alongside the houses and led to a detached garage in back. Most had been converted over to workshops, spare rooms, gyms, meth labs. That meant cars would make it off the street to the rear of the house, but rarely make it inside a garage. Ruby's car sat there looking at us over the chain link fence, a mid-nineties subcompact.

I tried to sit up, but it was a no go. Bricks helped me and leaned my back against something sturdy. "Car keys," I said. "Kitchen."

By the back door, a row of nails. Park the car, come in through the back door, hang your keys. Same routine for fifty years. Now, how Bricks was going to get inside a crime scene while the police were still working it was beyond me. But right then, most things were beyond me.

"Sit tight," she said. Like I had a choice. She stood and kept an eagle eye down the length of the driveway between houses. She made it to the fence and looked back at me where I was propped up against a planter. "It's good to see you," she said.

I smiled and gave her a thumb's up. She turned and I figured I'd be dead by the time she got back to me. Lifting my thumb took the last energy I had and I passed out again.

TWENTY-EIGHT
Bricks

I stood and watched the scene for at least ten minutes, running scenarios through my head. A single, bored cop stood at the back door of Aunt Ruby's house. He was supposed to be guarding the entrance, I'm sure, but what he was actually doing was goofing around on his phone.

Unfortunately, he wasn't distracted enough to slip by unseen, so if I went that route, I'd have to bluff him. But how? I was dressed in a touristy sweatshirt and dirty slacks. My cheek was swollen and had a small cut on it from Vito's pistol butt end. I didn't have anything close to a Boston accent, though that last obstacle was the smallest. I could probably fake it.

To what end? Pretend I was Internal Affairs or something? What if cops in this town mostly knew each other? Boston was a big city but if they used some sort of precinct system, it'd be like a bunch of small police departments, wouldn't it? People would know each other.

Shit. It didn't matter. Maybe if I was dressed in a sharp business suit and my face wasn't messed up. And if I had a fake badge. And a fake accent. But I was oh-for-four on any of those things.

I considered the front door but it was guarded, too, and most of the cops were in the entry way. Crime scene technicians were crawling all over the place, including the kitchen where the keys were hanging on a little hook. Or so Cam said. He was a little fucked up, so I couldn't even be sure the keys were there.

Maybe if I pretended to be a neighbor...?

And what? I was there to borrow some sugar? Ruby needed to return my casserole dish that I really needed right this second?

No.

This was a lost cause.

I went back to the neighbor's yard and shook Cam awake gently. He moaned, but his eyelids fluttered open.

"Come on," I said. "We've gotta get out of here."

"You get the keys?"

"Yeah," I said. "Right after I broke into Fort Knox, I stopped by and grabbed them."

He looked at me, confused. Obviously, sarcasm was above his functional level right now.

"Come on," I repeated, and helped him to his feet.

We made our way down the far side of the neighbor's house, our arms wrapped around each other like lovers, and turned away from Aunt Ruby's as soon as we hit the sidewalk. I expected to hear some cop's voice bellow after us in that distinct Boston accent, "Hey, you two! Come heah!"

But no one said a word.

We went around the corner and another half block before I started scanning the street. When I found an old Impala from somewhere in the 1970s, I used my elbow to push in a wing window and popped the lock. Quickly, I pushed Cam inside. He clambered clumsily past the steering wheel and collapsed on the passenger side.

I got in and closed the door.

"Cam."

"Whuh?"

"Cam, focus."

"Whuttizzit?"

"I need you to tell me how to hotwire this boat."

His eyes kicked open and he looked around the interior of the car. I waited patiently while he stared at the steering column for what seemed like an hour. We were sitting ducks in this car. If a neighbor or the car's owner looked out and saw us, they'd raise a hue and cry that would bring some curious cops from the next block over. That would not be good.

"Pop the column," Cam said, his voice a little steadier than before.

I followed his directions, and he walked me through the procedure as simply as if I was baking a cake. When the engine roared to life, I felt a small thrill go through me. I could almost understand why car thieves got off on this.

The sound made Cam smile, but then he leaned his head against the window and passed out.

I dropped the car into drive, and got us the hell out of there.

The doctor at the free clinic didn't once suggest we call the cops or go to the cops. He bought my superficial story that Cam and I were tourists who got mugged, or at least he pretended not to disbelieve it. He also surprised me by not trying to check me out first because I was a woman, but going straight for Cam due to his condition. Good to know chivalry didn't trump triage.

I sat nearby while the doctor stitched up Cam's wounds. He didn't ask any questions that weren't health related, and only one I didn't know the answer to.

"When did this other injury occur?"

"What other injury?"

He waved me over with his head, and nodded toward Cam's arm. I stared at the nasty cut with thick black stitching.

"I...I'm not sure."

The doctor pressed his lips together briefly. It was the closest thing to frustration he'd shown yet. Then he said, almost to himself, "Nice stitch work."

In the end, Cam got sewn up where he needed it, and he took some blood. We both got our wounds cleaned out. The doctor groused that they'd been dirty and were in danger of infection, so he prescribed some antibiotics. He provided us with plenty of Tylenol samples, too, which I was grateful for. He offered a prescription for something a little stronger, but I refused. It wasn't like we had time to stop at a pharmacy.

We were there for almost four hours, and in that time, Cam regained his bearings. He was still weak, but at least he was cognizant. When it was time to leave, I pulled out my wallet and held out everything I had left. The receptionist shook her head, pointing to the donation box. "Pay if you are able," she said. "We operate on grants and donations."

I slid the money into the box just as the doctor entered the room. "Thanks, Doc," I said.

"You both need rest," he told me.

"Good advice."

"And either a new line of work, or new hobbies," he

added. "Whatever it was that got you into this."

I nodded. Even better advice.

I left the Impala on the street. Cam and I took a slow walk until I found an ATM. We both withdrew the max allowable. My balance was under a grand, and when I asked Cam how he was looking for funds, he just frowned.

"Not good," he said.

"What about the last job? All they paid up front was the ten percent, right?"

He looked sheepish.

"Cam?"

"Yeah," he said. "We got the ten percent in cash. But I had them wire the balance to the offshore account. I figured it would be safer there, and we could transfer in some living expenses as needed."

I didn't reply.

"Sorry," he murmured.

"No," I said. "That was actually pretty smart. There's no way you could have known we'd have to lam it."

"The money's there," he said. "I checked the account on my computer before I left for Boston."

"Good."

"We can still get it."

"I know."

We were quiet for a little while, shuffling slowly down the sidewalk. Finally, Cam asked, "You said you saw Tia?"

"I had the pleasure, yeah."

"How was she?"

I glanced up at him. What was I supposed to say? That his girlfriend was a bitch who couldn't stand me? That she seemed to be schizophrenic about whether she cared about him or not?

"She told me about Aunt Ruby," I said.

"I got that. But how was she?"

I shrugged. "She was Tia. She hates me."

"Oh." He turned away. His shoulders slumped a little and his head hung.

I sighed. "Before I left, she asked me to do her a favor."

"A favor?"

"She asked me to take care of you."

That was like a shot in the arm. His shoulders squared, his chin raised, his shuffling step seemed more confident. Not for the first time, I wondered how that woman could be both poison and elixir at the same time.

I changed the subject. "I did some thinking while we were at the clinic."

"While I was bleeding, you were thinking. Teamwork."

"Yeah, so I was thinking about how you found your Aunt Ruby. I never even heard of her, but you found her."

"I probably never mentioned her. I barely even thought of her before Tia reminded me. It'd been forever since I'd seen her or my cousins."

"But they took you in. Hell, they fought by your side against Fazzio."

"That's family."

"That's what I thought, too. And that made me think of my Uncle Jack."

"Who's he?"

"He's my pop's brother. Left the city right after high school. Never got involved in the life. Him and Pops stayed in touch, but not very regularly."

"Where is he now?"

"Outside the city. He married a nice lady whose only dream was to own a bed and breakfast. They opened one up, and she died three years later. Last I heard, he still runs the place, though."

Cam thought about it. "You think he'd take us in?"

I shrugged. "He's family."

"Sounds good."

"The part about him taking us in was the good part. You ready for the bad part?"

He frowned. "No."

"Too bad. Here it is—the train only goes so far. To get to his little town, we've got to take the bus."

"Fuck," Cam muttered.

"Yeah."

The bus ride actually wasn't as bad as I thought. The coach we got on was never more than half full, and we sat somewhere in the middle the whole trip. Cam slept most of the way, and I picked up a paperback at the bus station and let my mind sink into the world of Lawrence Block.

When we arrived in the town where Uncle Jack lived, I marveled at the place. Here, less than three hours from the city, was small town America. The whole scene was like some kind of movie. I felt like a reverse rube—the city dweller shell shocked by Anytown, USA.

"It's nice," Cam said.

"Let's get a cab," I said.

Cam laughed. "Seriously?"

I frowned. He was probably right. Instead, I bought a

couple of Gatorades for us and got directions to the B&B from the grocer. Cam and I sipped the sports drinks and strolled down the idyllic streets.

"Not like it's even the same state, is it?" Cam said, his tone reverent.

"Not like it's the same fucking planet," I said.

"Yeah, but alien in a good way."

"Drink your Gatorade. You obviously need the electrolytes."

He smiled and took a sip, but his eyes were bright.

Jack's B&B was on a tree-lined street, of course. And it was white, with a nice front yard and a white picket fence. Of course. I knocked on the door, suddenly not sure if this was such a great idea. But when Jack opened the door, all my concerns faded.

"Paula?" His face was full of happy surprise. "My God, what are you doing here?"

"I was in the neighborhood."

He let out a roar of laughter and gave me a hard squeeze of a hug. I tried not to wince from the pain in my stomach. Then he swung open the front door. "Jesus, come in, come in."

And just like that, we were with family.

Jack didn't ask a lot of questions during our stay. At least, not the kind of questions I didn't feel like answering. It was probably a skill he learned from his relationship with Pops. What you don't know, you can't be asked to repeat to the feds. He probed a little bit about Cam and me but we kept it vague, and he didn't pry too much. When we first arrived, he had a full slate of guests except for one room, and when he asked if one room would do, neither of us balked.

We ate a good dinner along with the other five guests. I could feel the sidelong glances at my face and Cam's injuries, but we politely deflected questions and focused on the food. Jack was either a great cook or he employed one. The meal was straight meat and potatoes fare, but that was exactly what we both needed.

Before I headed up to the room, I asked Jack for an extra blanket and pillow. He handed them to me without a word, but then he asked me if I'd have a nightcap with him. I'd passed up the wine at dinner, but right about then, a drink sounded pretty good.

We sat at the kitchen table and he poured us each some whiskey. "Ice?" he asked.

I shrugged. "However you take it is fine."

He handed me a glass. "I like it neat," he said. "But Linda always took it on the rocks."

I didn't know what to say to that, so I settled for sipping my drink.

Jack did the same, seeming to savor the whiskey. I'd never acquired a discerning taste for the stuff myself, but I knew some people were into it just like wine snobs were into the vino. When he finished, he glanced over at me. "You know, I really am glad to see you, Paula."

"Thanks," I said.

"I mean it."

"I believe you. Thanks for taking us in."

He took another sip, savored it like the first. Then he said, "I regret all the time I missed with Antonio, and you."

"You had your life, he had his." I shrugged. "I've got mine."

"True," he admitted. "But I still wish..."

"What?"

He shrugged. "What is it they say? That it is foolish to try to reorder a life already lived?"

I smiled. My Uncle Jack was a philosopher. Maybe that's where I got it from. It was genetic.

"What's so funny?"

"You sound like one of my college profs."

"Yeah? What's your degree?"

"Philosophy."

He smiled, too. Then his smile faded a little. "I'm really glad to see you, Paula. And you can stay here as long as you need to. But I just have to know one thing."

"Sure."

"I know this isn't just a visit for the sake of reuniting with long lost family." He motioned towards the bruising on my face.

I shrugged. "Not exactly."

"The problems that brought you here, I need to know they're not going to follow you. Because this place, it's all I've got left of Linda and our life together. I don't want it...sullied. You follow me?"

"Yeah, Uncle Jack, I do. And I promise you, nothing will follow us here. More than that, we'll be out of your hair as soon as we're strong enough."

He waved his hand. "Stay as long as you want, as long as it's just the two of you. No trouble."

"No trouble," I repeated.

We finished our drinks, and I headed up to bed, hoping to Christ I was right about that.

***

I thought things would be awkward with Cam, but I should have known better. He offered to take the couch, but I refused. "You're banged up worse than I am. You need the rest more."

He didn't argue. We took turns undressing to our undergarments and cleaning each other's wounds. I felt like we were a pair of baboons grooming each other, but it was easier than cleaning our own injuries.

"That's nasty," Cam said as he wiped the cut on my belly. "What happened?"

"Bruno's cousin tried to give me an emergency C-section."

He grimaced. "His cousin?"

I realized how little we'd talked since he crawled out of the doghouse in Boston. We spent the next hour relating our respective experiences while cleaning up the painful results of those same experiences.

"A tailor?" I asked him. "Dude, that's hard core."

He grinned sheepishly. "Adapt and overcome, right?"

I nodded, a little proud of him. "Exactly."

After we were both cleaned up and had swallowed some Tylenol, we tried to sleep. On the couch, I hovered right on the edge, my mind not wanting to completely let go. I had visions of Vito Taggliarti and a couple of Fazzio's thugs busting in through the bedroom door.

"Bricks?"

"Yeah?"

"Now what?"

"Now we sleep."

"I can't."

"Why not?"

"Same reason I'm betting you can't. Because my mind keeps asking, now what?"

I thought about it for a few seconds. Then I asked, "What do you want to do?"

His response was immediate. "Kill that fucker Fazzio. Senior, I mean."

"All right, then. That's what we'll do."

"Good."

Somehow, just saying that made things better. My vigilance softened and I drifted down into sleep. I don't know if it was only a few seconds or several minutes before Cam spoke again, rousing me out of the beginnings of a dream.

"Bricks?"

"What?"

"What about after?"

"After what?"

"After we kill Fazzio. What, then?"

I blinked wearily, and fell back on the same question I'd used before. "What do you want to do?"

He chuckled ruefully. "Ride off into the sunset with Tia. But that ain't happening."

I was too exhausted to argue the point, and wouldn't have anyway. He was probably right.

"Then what?" I asked, my voice slurred with sleep.

He sighed deeply. "Boston will be a dead town to us after Fazzio, if it isn't already. And it sounds like home is going to be too dangerous, too."

"Probably."

"So what does that leave?"

I took in a deep breath, trying to clear my thoughts

from the sleepy fog that was descending on me. Finally, I said, "Tell you what. Let's take care of Fazzio. We need to be focused to make that work. And then, we'll worry about after."

He didn't answer. I started drifting back down into blissful rest again. At some point, I think I heard him say, "Sounds like a plan," but I could have been dreaming that.

TWENTY-NINE
Cameron

A week later I didn't care if I ever saw a city again. I'd never understood the appeal of the whole ditch-it-all-open-a-B&B thing before, but I was really starting to get it after some time with Uncle Jack.

If it weren't for that nagging itch in the back of my brain like a tick burrowed in there growing fat on the blood. I still had Fazzio Sr. looming and he'd still tried to kill me. That's not something I could ever leave behind, no matter how beautiful the scenery.

The other thing nagging at me was Tia. It had been a week—nine days, actually. I'd nearly died in Boston and while I appreciated that she gave Bricks what little information she did, Tia hadn't come to see me when I was only a bus ride away. I knew why. It was her fear and hatred of the life and everything associated with it. I could imagine the look in her eye if she saw me and saw my wounds—the fault line scar running from elbow to wrist, the slice in my side, the nicks and cuts on my face like I'd spent years shaving with a dull rock. If she saw all that in person she'd have to confront who I was again. And for her, it was easier living in denial.

And forget telling her what I knew we had to do next. If I told her we were going back to Boston, running straight at the man who'd hung me out a window, she'd give me that quiet head shake and the silent tears that crawled down her face in slow motion.

She may not have needed stitches, but she was hurting every time she looked at me. Our history and what I'd done to get rid of her boyfriend couldn't ever cover that hurt. I'd never get used to her looks the same way she'd never get used to me walking out the door on a job.

The best thing for her, and for me, was to let her go.

I bet it was the tall trees, the greenery, the birds and the frogs at night. The quiet that isn't quiet, but it isn't traffic and sirens and arguments on the streets in some language you've never heard. People in the city think the country is all silence, but it's not. It's just a different kind of noise. It didn't put me on edge the same way, a way I'd grown up with and thought I needed to survive.

God, I was sounding like some kind of fruitcake. Fact is though, I knew it was right to break it off with Tia and I came to that decision walking by a creek while a woodpecker sounded overhead. Go figure.

So I called her.

"I'm not coming back," I said.

"What do you mean?" There was hurt in her voice, but also hope.

"Exactly that. I still have some things to do and then after that, I don't know what. But I'm not coming back." I paused and she waited for me to say more. "I guess though, to really answer your question, what I mean is...you're free. You don't owe me anything. You don't have to worry about me anymore."

"Cam, I—" She stopped there. I didn't know what words stuck in her throat, whether something she knew I didn't want to hear or something she couldn't bring herself to say.

"It's all right. If you could pack up my things. I'll send for them. I'm not sure when."

"Are you gonna be okay?"

"You know me. I'll make out all right."

"Cam, you know it's not you, right? It's the job."

"I am the job, Tia. The job is me." I'd never felt that to be more true. "Goodbye. For what it's worth, I'll probably always love you."

I hung up before she could say anything else.

At dinner Bricks could tell I was in a mood. The other people staying at the B&B were always talky and friendly. Never my scene in the best of moods, but I really kept to myself that night.

We always helped Jack clear the tables seeing as we weren't paying him anything to stay there. Bricks and I had time to talk over a steaming sink of dirty dishes.

"So you gonna tell me or what?" she said.

Resistance was futile. "I broke it off with Tia."

She let the water run a while before saying anything. I rinsed coffee mugs, stacked dessert plates. "She never came to see you."

"Couldn't handle it, I guess."

"I guess. Not many people could."

"I see now why you never go on dates." As soon as I said it I felt like I crossed some sort of line. It was shitty thing to say. "Bricks, I'm sorry. I didn't mean—"

"You're right," she said. "I know you can't get serious with someone doing what we do. It never works. So why try?"

She took the plate from my hand and ran the drying

towel over it, set it on the stack with the others. We finished the job with nothing but the chiming of silverware to fill the quiet.

Another week and I could move almost like I had before. Jack gave us the address to a free clinic in town and I went in to get my stitches removed. The nurse who did it had a lot of questions about my arm and why there seemed to be threads from an Italian suit instead of an ER in my skin, but I played dumb and said that's what the doctor had given me. I played it off that I was in a rural part of New Hampshire when the camping accident occurred. The little holes where the thread had been wept blood when she pulled them out.

Bricks and I both felt it was getting close to time for us to pull out and finish what we started. We hadn't talked much about what came after, but focus on the target was our priority.

I couldn't tell her how to find the office where they first brought me. In all that confusion and at night those North End streets all looked the same to me. I could go back to Vincent, but after I'd brought death right to Aunt Ruby's door I was reluctant to ask anything more of the old man. And I had no idea what happened to Tag and Boyd after the shootout at their house. I'd seen Boyd get hit with a flesh wound, but their fate could be in the hands of the cops, in which case the Boston PD probably had my description. They certainly had my blood from the scene, but chances were good they couldn't tell whose blood was whose in that mess.

One thing Bricks made clear early on was that nothing

come back to Uncle Jack, so I didn't even want to call Ruby's old number in case the boys had moved back in. One trace from the cops or from Fazzio could mean a repeat of Ruby's last stand down here in God's country. And Jack wasn't even in the life.

Bricks, though, had a damn good idea. She called around and did a little Internet research to find out where Fazzio Jr's funeral had taken place. From the news reports it was a big affair, heavily attended by wise guys and cops alike. He was buried in a big marble mausoleum next to his mother and grandparents, and the funeral home was easy to find.

She called.

"Yeah, I was unable to attend the Fazzio funeral and I wanted to pay my respects. Can you tell me where to send flowers to the elder Mr. Fazzio."

She waited a moment then nodded and started writing down an address the dumb schmuck on the other end was giving her. When she'd hung up Bricks had written out our last hit list, and it was a short one. Only one name, and exactly where to find him.

THIRTY
Bricks

Saying goodbye to Uncle Jack was harder than I expected. In what must have looked like a Monty Python skit, I actually offered my hand to him as he reached for a hug. That threw him off, and he fumbled to adjust. About that time, I decided a hug was more the order of things, so I opened my arms and leaned in. The hand he clumsily extended hit me right in the boob.

A little awkward, yeah.

But Jack just laughed it off and wrapped his arms around me in a big bear hug. He told me he loved me and he squeezed for a long while. That part wasn't awkward. Not even a little bit.

The funny thing about staying at Jack's B&B was even though he was insanely different than my pops, and completely his own person, every once in a while some gesture or turn of phrase would leak out that reminded me they were brothers. So while I really enjoyed getting to know Jack for who he was, I also got small reminders of my pops. And that was nice.

"You come back and see me," Jack said in my ear. "We're family. We should see each other sometimes."

"I will," I promised, though I didn't know if it was a promise I could keep.

After Jack released me from his hug, he turned to Cam. Cam stuck out his hand and Jack reluctantly took it, probably figuring he didn't have the family card to play for an upgrade to a hug. But he pumped Cam's hand repeatedly, and told him he was glad to know him.

"Thanks, Uncle Jack," Cam said, then actually blushed a little. "I mean Jack. Sorry."

"No, no. Uncle Jack it is." Jack winked at him. "You're welcome here, too, Cameron. Any time."

We thanked him again, and then took the long, beautiful walk to the bus stop.

On the ride back to New York, we finally started to plan in earnest. Since the entire middle third of the bus was empty, we didn't have to do much more than keep our voices low in order to keep it a private conversation.

"We've got the address," Cam said. "We should just sneak in and clip him."

"We've got his home address," I said. "Which means guards and alarms and who knows what else."

"His home is the perfect place to off him. After what he did to Aunt Ruby..."

"I hear you." I lifted my purse. "But we've got my .45 with three mags, and the gun I took off the goombah at RACKS 11, which is a .40 with just the one mag in it. We need more firepower, or at least more ammo."

Cam thought about it. "I've got another pistol in the safe at Tia's place. And ammo."

"I know. And I've got ten boxes of .45 rounds at my apartment, plus a shotgun. But none of that does us any good."

He gave me a doubtful expression. "You really think they're still staking us out?"

"I would."

"Yeah, but it's been over three weeks. At some point, they've got to give up."

"Maybe. But we're not just talking Fazzio's people. Trepani could be looking for me, too. Taking a chance that one boss decided to pull the plug on surveillance after a week is risky enough. Betting that both of them did? Bad odds."

"If they were even staking us out at all," Cam argued, but I could tell he didn't really believe it. He was just looking for the easiest solution to our problem.

"That's the problem. We don't know. And if we're wrong, we end up in a fight we don't need at a time we don't want it. And if it's Fazzio, then he's tipped off to us. We lose our element of surprise."

Cam sighed. "Yeah, you're right. I was just playing the devil's advocate, you know?"

"Well, put your pitchfork away and let's figure this out. Can you get to our offshore money?"

"Yeah," he said. "Now that I don't look like I'm in the middle of a *Die Hard* sequel, I can actually go into a bank and get it wired."

"How long will it take?"

"Couple of hours."

"All right. That'll be your mission. Get the money, and meet me."

"How much?"

"How much do we have?"

He shrugged. "Maybe fifteen."

"You know what? Get it all. What we don't spend on guns, we'll need to travel on."

"Got it." He snorted and shook his head. "My life's

work, and all I'll have to show for it is an empty offshore account."

"You've got life," I said. "You can't put a value on that."

I don't know for sure if I was being serious or sarcastic or a little of both, but neither of us spoke for a while after that. We rode in silence, and thought about what I'd said. Or at least, that's what I did. From the look on Cam's face, I'm guessing he was, too.

We splurged for a hotel room a cut above the hot sheet special or the roach-infested inn. While I waited for Cam to make it back with our cash, I made a couple of calls to get us some weapons. Before I had the trouble with Trepani, there were a half dozen or more people I could have got in touch with, even to the point of playing them off of each other to get a better deal. But now I needed to stick with smaller independents who may not know about what happened at RACKS 11 or didn't care. Of course, that turned things into more of a seller's market.

In the end, it was Asian Andy who agreed to meet me. I don't know why they called him that, since his skin was pale and his hair red. Maybe it was because he dealt in Chinese AK-47s instead of Russian ones. Maybe it was because he lived in an apartment in Chinatown. At this point, I didn't care. I was just glad he had some inventory he was willing to part with.

Cam returned with three envelopes of five grand each. We stuffed one apiece in our waistbands, and I put the third one in my pocket. Andy had always been straight, so I wasn't too worried about a rip-off, but you never knew.

"I want a .44 Magnum," Cam said.

"Look at you. Dirty Harry."

He shook his head. "Nah. Aunt Ruby gave me one back at her house when Fazzio, Jr. showed up. I liked the feel of it."

"It's a solid weapon."

"I'm not trying to be Clint Eastwood or anything."

"Right," I said and smiled at him. We both knew that's exactly who he wanted to be.

The warehouse was on the outskirts of an industrial district. We'd met there once before, so I knew the way. The cab driver seemed a little skittish about the area, and I couldn't blame him. Benjamin Franklin helped convince him, though.

Andy didn't have as much stock as he usually did, but other than that, things were pretty normal. He laid out several handguns, a shotgun, and two rifles. The rifles were Kalashnikovs, which blew my Asian Andy nickname theory all to hell.

"These are out of my price range right now," I told him, pushing the rifles aside.

"No worries," Andy said.

Cam grinned in delight and held up a .44 Magnum revolver. It didn't have as long a barrel as the prototypical Dirty Harry model, and it was stainless steel instead of blued, but that didn't seem to matter.

I hovered over the shotgun, but the whole concealment thing made me decide to pass. The best choice turned out to be the simplest. I stocked up on ammo for my .45, and traded Andy the goombah's .40 cal straight across for a small .380 that I could hide pretty much anywhere on my body.

Cam grabbed a box of .44 shells to go with his find. I pointed to another small pistol. "He needs a backup."

Andy picked up the small gun. "A .25, Bricks? Not much in the way of firepower."

"Better than nothing at all."

"Barely." He held up the .25 auto. "You shoot someone with this, you need to be careful, huh?"

"Why's that?"

"Because they might find out you shot them, and get a little pissed about it."

"That bad, huh?"

He half shrugged, half nodded.

"Why're you selling it, if it sucks so much?"

"There's a market for everything," Andy said. "This here, I'd say the target demographic is someone with an extreme need to hide their piece, and someone who is going to do their business up close." He shrugged again. "Or a lady."

I gave him a dark look, but without any real conviction behind it.

He held up a hand. "I don't mean you, Bricks. You're..."

"I'm what?"

"A professional," he said. "Different rules for pros."

"Ah."

He picked up a five-shot .38 that was hammerless. "Here. This is the shit."

Cam took the gun, cracked open the cylinder and snapped it shut again. "Yeah?"

"Hey, ten thousand cops can't be wrong, right?"

Cam nodded in agreement and put the pistol in the small of his back. I marveled at the exchange. My partner and fellow button man just took the advice of an illicit arms dealer based upon the implicit recommendation of the country's largest police department.

The world is a funny place sometimes.

I paid Andy without haggling. He went his way and we went ours. The cabbie was definitely pleased to be leaving the area. Once we were back on an arterial and headed toward civilization again, the driver asked us where we wanted to go. I directed him to the train station.

We bought our train tickets, found our seats, and sat back to enjoy the ride to Boston. Once we were underway, I turned to Cam. "What do you think? You want to rest up first, or head straight over?"

His expression was difficult to read. "I...there's someplace I want to go first."

"Where's that?"

He told me, and it made perfect sense.

THIRTY-ONE
Cameron

Call it unfinished business, call it guilt, but I wanted to visit Ruby's gravesite. Bricks had actually given me the idea when she called about Fazzio's funeral. It was the first time I realized, shit, Aunt Ruby had one of those too. A pang of guilt throbbed in my gut.

I knew we'd be on a fast track to leave town after the job with Fazzio was done so I wanted to get this out of the way so we could high-tail it out of Boston before the body cooled. I copied Bricks' trick with the funeral home, though it took three tries to get the right place. I just started calling the ones closest to her house and kept calling, skipping over the Jewish one.

She'd been cremated and interred in a big marble structure in a cemetery in one of the suburbs. We rented a car. Better than being beholden to cab drivers if we needed to get lost fast.

I drove and Bricks and I spent most of the time in our usual silence. It's part of what made us good partners. We didn't do small talk. I went for some big talk right then.

"So, let's say I'd died..."

"Yeah," she said warily.

"Would you have handled my funeral?"

"Depends."

"On what?"

"Well," she said, turning in her seat a little to parse it out. "If you died in the shootout at Ruby's—"

"Makes it sound like a western movie."

She didn't laugh at my interruption. "If you'd died there then the cops would have your body. I'm not family so I can't do a formal identification and I doubt they'd release the body to me. Plus, they'd want to ask a whole lot of questions and I'd rather keep my name out of a situation like that."

"Makes sense."

"And even if I was able to get your body from the morgue, I don't know what you want done with it. Do you have a plot? A family thing somewhere? Do you want to be cremated? Want me to scatter your ashes at sea or something like that?"

"I don't really like boats, so no." We drove on a while longer, each thinking our own thoughts. "I guess we should have a plan for that scenario, huh?"

"Yeah, maybe."

The thing that really struck me—I didn't have anyone else I could think of to handle it. With Tia out of my life now, Bricks was as close to family as I had. The thought depressed me, if I'm honest. Nothing against Bricks, I just felt like my life added up to more but there I was staring at the equation and the answer was one. One friend. One person close to me. One person I could trust.

I had to think she was sitting there next to me thinking the same damn thing.

When we got to the cemetery the sky had clouded over like my thoughts. I found her little plaque next to where her ashes were interred, just one of a hundred little cubby-holes sealed behind a slab on this wall, with dozens more walls in the marble lined building. The place called for quiet, but every step you took echoed and every cough seemed to amplify off the stone walls and floors. Bricks hung back a few yards and let me have my moment.

In my head I apologized to Ruby. Too little, too late. I looked down the row of brass plaques and wondered if anyone else in there had died with a double barrel shotgun sizzling in their hands.

There was a little vase next to each marble rectangle in the wall. Most were empty, but the newer ones, the plaques less tarnished, held some flowers. Aunt Ruby's had a little trio of roses, not enough to call a bouquet. Curious, I looked at the card attached. They were from Tag. No note, just FROM TAG TO RUBY. Then a business card for the florist and the receipt. Yeah, the numbskull left the price tag on his funeral flowers.

Seven dollars for the flowers, twelve for the delivery fee which seemed a little extreme to me. Then an address and phone number. Tag's place. I slipped the scrap of paper out and put it in my pocket. I couldn't apologize properly to Aunt Ruby, but maybe I could to Tag. And I could find out what happened to Boyd.

"You don't have to come with me," I told Bricks as we drove away from the cemetery.

"No, I'll go. What else am I gonna do?" That one hung in the air for a while, then Bricks said, "Shit, sorry, Cam. That sounded cold. I'll go with you because I want to. You know what I meant, right?"

"I did. Don't worry about it."

The sheet of gray overhead followed us into the city and flattened all the light. Beside me Bricks shifted in her seat. She was acting like a kid who had to piss. I felt like an idiot asking a grown woman if I needed to pull over, but it dawned on me what was really going on.

"You don't want to stop and see Tag, do you?"

She gave me a guilty smile. "To be honest, Cam, I'd rather get this over with." Meaning Fazzio Sr.

"I know. But this is something I feel like I have to do. This trip feels like I'm cutting some ties, y'know?"

"I know. I feel it too. That part of me isn't anxious at all to get it done because I don't know what comes next. I feel like going far away. Like west coast or something. Not running." She made her point with a firm finger in the air. Bricks wasn't usually one for the typical Italian hand acrobatics while she talked so I knew she wanted to make a point here. "We're not running away, just making a new start."

"I hear you," I said. "It won't take long. Then we'll get to Fazzio and get the hell out of Massachusetts and go as far away as we need to."

The rental car GPS told me where to get off the highway.

"You ever drive cross country?" she asked.

"No. You?"

"No. I've barely been out of New England."

"Seems like something you do in your early-twenties."

"Yeah."

But right then we were both feeling the call of the open road.

Tag lived like a bachelor. His apartment was on the second floor of a three-story brick building. I knocked and waited, Bricks a few steps back over my shoulder.

When the door opened I thought Tag was going to break into a run the other direction.

"You're alive," he said like he wanted to confirm what his eyes were telling him.

"Yeah. Barely." I gestured over my shoulder. "This is Bricks...uh, Paula."

Tag didn't acknowledge her. "Shit, man. We thought you were dead."

"Yeah, well, according to the files I think I am. I'm gonna use that to my advantage and split town. I really wanted to come by and say I'm sorry."

Tag waited, stone faced, for more.

"So..." I said. "I'm really sorry."

"That's it?"

I glanced over my shoulder to Bricks to see if I was missing something. "Yeah. Sorry."

"Mom is dead. Boyd *almost* died. And you're sorry?" His eyes had gone from confused to steel hard.

"Tag, what else do you want?" It started to become obvious he hadn't let us in and I really didn't want to hash this out in the hallway.

"I don't know what else, but Jesus fuck, Cam, that's all you can say?"

"What else is there? I went to Ruby's...to the cemetery. I paid my respects."

He was getting agitated now. It felt like a meeting with a displeased boss, or maybe an angry wife. "And you think that lets you off the hook?"

"What hook? Look, I know the whole thing got a little fucked up—"

"A little?" He flung his hands up and rolled his neck in a wide act of disbelief.

"Okay, a lot. But it's really Fazzio's fault."

Tag stepped forward and thrust an angry finger at me. "Fazzio has been here since before I was born and there's never been any trouble. You show up and two days later the fucking sky is falling."

"Hey, kid." Bricks stepped up closer behind me. "It's not Cam's fault. If these assholes hadn't started this shit in the first place—"

"Pardon me," Tag said. "But I don't even know who the fuck you are, so butt out, lady."

If only Tag knew Bricks was packing, and how easily she could draw down on him. But I knew. I held out an open hand to each of them like I was trying to head off a bar fight before it started.

"Relax, Tag. Leave her out of it."

A sleepy voice spoke from behind Tag. "What's going on?"

Boyd appeared looking tired and worn. Thinner than when I saw him last, but alive.

"Boyd, good to see you," I said."

"Holy shit," he said, coming more awake. "You motherfucker."

Now I started to get annoyed. "Hey, I fought like hell and killed a whole lot of guys for you. Things could have been worse."

"Yeah," Tag said. "You could have died. That would have been tragic."

His sarcasm came on thicker in that deep Boston accent of his.

I put a hand on my hip and turned to Bricks again for support. Her face told me all she was thinking was I told you so. No help there. I didn't want to leave it this way.

Second cousins, third cousins, whatever they were—this was still family. But I guess it wouldn't be the first time I'd been disowned by my own blood. I had to count the fact they weren't trying to kill me as a step up in family relations.

I had an idea. A stupid idea, but one I thought might work. I took the envelope of cash from my pocket and handed over the five grand I'd been carrying since we emptied out our accounts.

"Here," I said, slapping the envelope into Tag's hands. "Take this. It'll cover Ruby's funeral, maybe some of Boyd's medical costs."

"What is that? Money?" Boyd asked.

"Cam, what are you doing?" Bricks wanted to know.

I held out a pacifying hand to her. "It's my share, not yours."

"To these guys?" She couldn't believe me. I guess I couldn't either, really, but it seemed like the right thing to do.

I turned back to Tag at the door. "Take it. You earned it. And if it makes you feel any better, you'll never see me again."

"I don't know if we'd survive it if we did." Tag tightened his fist around the envelope and slammed the door in my face.

I stood there for a few seconds a little stunned. A pang of regret seeped in, but I told myself until I believed it that I'd done the right thing. It would make starting over a little harder, but doing things the hard way was my M.O.

I turned away from the door and into Brick's displeased stare.

"Fuck it," I said. "Let's go finish this."

THIRTY-TWO
Bricks

Someone once said it's hard to stay mad at someone when you love them. I'd like to meet that person and kick their ass. Because that person is an idiot.

I love Cam. He's something more than a brother, more than a colleague, more than a fellow stranded traveler on this journey of life. It's not even close to romantic, either. Maybe it has something to do with shared experience, but probably it is mostly about understanding. We understand what the other has been through. We understand each other. And we care. If that's not love, I don't know what it is.

But love or not, it didn't keep me from wanting to box his fucking ears.

I kept silent in the car, mostly to avoid blowing up at him. But he couldn't leave well enough alone.

"I handled the situation," he said, his voice even but tinged with the slightest bit of an entreaty.

"You sure did," I replied through gritted teeth.

"He was a mess."

"Clearly."

"Both of them were. And it was my fault."

"It was Fazzio's fault."

"No," he said. "They got involved because of me. And getting involved cost them. A lot."

"They made their own choices," I told him.

"They did it because I was family. They barely knew

me, but..." His eyes misted slightly and his voice turned thick.

"They weren't civilians, those two," I said easily. "Not from what you told me."

"They were just tough kids. Boston kids, from the neighborhood." He shrugged. "I guess I'm just tired of the collateral damage, Bricks. The people who we take out deserve it. They're in the life, or they make a big mistake. But the ones that get caught in the crossfire..."

My anger deflated. I knew what he meant. I'd felt the same way more than once.

I...understood.

Besides, I had exactly one friend left in the world. How much time was I going to spend being mad at him over five large?

"I get it," I said, my tone softer. "Don't worry about it."

"Thanks." He put his hand on my shoulder, gave it a squeeze, and let go.

I shrugged, and drove on in silence. Then a small inspiration struck.

"Maybe we can score some road money from Fazzio." I glanced over at him. "The guy has to have some cash around the house."

Cam smiled. "You never know."

It turned out that Fazzio owned a large brownstone on Beacon Hill. We circled through the neighborhood slowly, finally parking a half block away. I wanted to be within sprinting distance of the car when we were finished.

Cam chuckled and shook his head.

"What?"

He motioned at the houses. "All these gangsters, as soon as they make some serious money, what do they want to do? Get accepted by the legitimate crowd. Like that will ever happen."

I edged back the slide of my .45. A glint of brass showed in the chamber. "Sure it will."

"No way," Cam said. "These society people will never accept a Fazzio, just like no one in the city would accept a Giordano."

"It takes a generation," I said. "See, what happens is that these guys get their money together, and then they legitimize most of it. Once it's honest money, it takes about a generation for these society mopes to go from thinking they're trashy criminals to having a cool cachet."

Cam opened his .44, checked his ammo load, then spun the cylinder and flicked it back into place. It was a simple move, but a confident one.

Good, I thought. One more dance for Slaughterhouse.

"They'll always look down their nose at new money," he said.

"JFK's pop made his money bootlegging. It didn't even take a generation for him to be seen as respectable. And he put his son in the White House."

"Yeah?" He thought about it for a second. "Well, I'll tell you one thing Bostonians don't have to worry about."

I knew where he was going, but I waited anyway. I even gave him an expectant expression to play off of.

Cam smiled. "President Fazzio."

We got out of the car and strolled past Fazzio's place. There were no guards out front, but I saw a shadow inside the outer door. It could have been a doorman, but my guess was that in Fazzio's world, doormen were armed to the teeth.

There was no proper alley behind the brownstone, just a narrow walkway between Fazzio's place and the back of the home on the next street over. If either of us were even reasonably good at parkour, scaling the wall would be an option. I wondered if Fazzio kept the windows on this side of the house locked.

"Here's where we could use that rope you were talking about," Cam muttered, his thoughts obviously going along the same lines.

I stared up at the windows. "How far apart do you think those windows are?

He stared for a moment, calculating. "Maybe...six feet?"

"I've got an idea."

The toughest part was making sure we got the right house. No one answered the door. I looked for any sign of an alarm system but didn't see one. B&E wasn't my specialty by a long stretch, though, so it was a risk.

"If the alarm goes off, we gotta work fast," I said.

"How will we know? It could be silent."

I shrugged. "Proceed as if."

"Got it."

I waited until the coast was as clear as it was going to get, then smashed the glass panel next to the door handle. The only sound that greeted me was the clattering of broken glass chunks to the floor. I reached through and popped open the deadbolt. We stepped quickly inside and closed the door behind us.

Cam was already moving through the luxurious home, looking for what we needed. Out of habit, I flipped the deadbolt back into place and started my own search. All the while, I kept my eyes open for any flashing red lights or other indicators of an alarm. The last thing I wanted to deal with right now was the Boston PD.

It took Cam all of two minutes to find an expandable step-ladder. “It was in the utility closet off the kitchen,” he said, his tone hushed. “It goes up to eight feet.”

“Nice work.”

We made our way up the stairs and to the rear of the house and picked a window. The corresponding window in Fazzio’s place had open drapes, and it looked like it could be a den or maybe even an office.

Carefully, we opened the window and stretched the ladder out toward the opposite ledge.

It didn’t reach.

“Shit,” I muttered.

We pulled it back and Cam adjusted the length to its full eight feet. Then he glanced at me. “I hope it’s enough.”

“Only one way to know.”

We extended the ladder out again. At first, it was light, but every foot away from us made it heavier and heavier. Sweat popped up on my forehead and my forearms started to ache. When the top of the ladder bumped up against the ledge across the way, I almost let out a small victory yell.

It took a little more jostling, but we managed to get the ladder solidly butted up against the opposite window while leaving a couple of inches of the ladder foot on the near side ledge. It certainly wasn't going to pass any OSHA standards, but it might work.

I slid my gun into my belt and started to climb onto the ledge. Cam stopped me.

"I'll go first," he said.

"I'm lighter."

"Maybe, but not by much. Besides, this is my thing. We're here because of me. I'll go first."

I shrugged and moved aside.

Tentatively, Cam climbed up on the ledge. He hesitated, as if steeling his resolve, but once he started, he scurried across our little bridge in one continuous, smooth motion. I watched the ladder shift a little with his movements, and bow noticeably downward when he was in the middle of his trip, but it held up.

As soon as he reached the window, he peered in cautiously, then pushed up on the bottom pane.

It slid open easily.

Cam shot me a grin before he clambered inside of Fazzio's house.

"Son of a bitch," I breathed.

I steadied myself on the ledge, took a deep breath, and began crawling across the ladder. It seemed to move and shift more than it did for Cam. A brisk wind blew upward, biting into all the areas I was sweating. I shivered, but kept shimmying across.

When I felt the center give slightly, bowing downward, I made the mistake of looking down. While my brain told me I was only one story up, my eyes argued that it was about a mile down to the ground. The unpleasant image of a watermelon splatting on the asphalt below flitted through my mind.

I looked away, and kept crawling.

Cam stood in the window, his hands extended toward me. Excitement shone in his eyes. The kid was in his element now.

As I neared the edge of the Fazzio's window, my knee missed a rung and slipped into the space in between. That caused me to lurch to the right, and my body weight pulled the ladder with me. I heard the foot end, now disproportionately lightened with me at the other end, skip across the window ledge, then fall silent. I knew what was coming.

The goddamn watermelon, that's what.

I lashed out with both hands, grabbing for Fazzio's ledge. Instead, I caught both of Cam's hands at the wrists.

The ladder spun sideways and fell without a sound until it clattered to the asphalt below. I was surprised at how little noise it made, but given how much adrenaline was shooting through my bloodstream, maybe my hearing was off.

Cam gripped my wrists tightly, but I was sweaty and knew that grip would start to slip. I held on for all I was worth and tried to pull myself up.

"Your legs," Cam grunted. "Use your legs."

How the fuck...?

Then I got it.

I planted my feet against the side of the building and used the resistance to pull against. Cam pulled at the same time, and I came up a good six or eight inches. I took a step along the wall and we heaved upward another six or so.

On the next step, I could feel the slipperiness of my hands start to slide.

Cam must have felt it, too. "One last big one," he said.

I pushed off with my feet and pulled with my aching arms. Thank God he made his move at the same time or I might have simply yanked him right out of the window and we'd both have fallen down on top of that fucking ladder. That'd make for a nice couple of column inches on the police blotter of the *Boston Herald* under the headline about idiot criminals.

But he did pull at the same time, heaving backward with all his might and actually falling over onto his ass.

I landed with my gut on the center of the ledge, getting a little of the wind knocked out of me in the process.

Believe me, it was worth it.

I slid the rest of the way into the room, and we sat there for a few moments, catching our breath.

"Je-zus," Cam muttered.

"Thanks," I whispered back.

He nodded. "You still got your gun?"

I felt for my .45 and found the reassuring weight of it in the small of my back. "Still there."

Cam stood. "You ready?"

I dried my palms on my pant legs, then joined him. "Fuck, yeah."

The room was obviously Fazzio's home office. The drapes may have been open now, but they were dark red and thick, so it would have been easy for him to get one hundred percent privacy if he ever needed it. I don't know how much dirty work a guy like that chooses to do in his own home, but I admired the fact he was prepared either way. That'd probably turn out to be the only thing I admired about the guy.

Cam opened the door slowly, and we scouted the hallway. It was empty, but in the distance, I could hear human activity. It sounded like the light drone of a vacuum cleaner or electric sweeper, probably coming from downstairs.

We moved as quietly as we could, searching the upstairs room by room. There were two bathrooms, a spare bedroom, and Fazzio's opulent master suite. All were empty. We regrouped near his office. Heading downstairs was the only option at this point, but it was going to be tricky. We knew there were people there, but hopefully we could pick them off one at a time. As soon as things got noisy, we'd be facing the entire cavalry.

"Maybe we should split up," Cam whispered.

I shook my head. "No, we need to stick together."

"What if—"

The clacking sound of footsteps on the stairs interrupted him. I jerked my head to Fazzio's office and we slipped inside. The steps grew nearer, so we took up positions on opposite sides of the door. When the door swung open, a bull of a man stepped through. He wore a nice suit and moved with the easy grace of an athlete. He stiffened when he saw the open window.

I pressed the barrel of my .45 against the back of his skull before he could react further. "Easy now," I said in a low voice. "Or I'll spatter your brains all over that expensive suit."

He slowly raised his hands to shoulder level.

"Take two steps forward," I ordered.

He did, not looking over his shoulder at me. I moved

with him, keeping my .45 leveled at his head.

Cam closed the door quietly, then checked the guy for weapons. He found a pistol under his left shoulder. Cam pushed it into his own belt, then turned to the windows and drew the drapes on all but the open one.

"Knees, big guy," I said.

The bodyguard slowly lowered himself to one knee, then the other.

Cam took a seat on the edge of Fazzio's desk. He peered into the man's face with an intensity I hadn't seen very often. He was in full Slaughterhouse mode. "Where is Fazzio? Watching TV downstairs? Plowing the housekeeper? Huh? Where is he?"

"He's not home," the man grunted. He had a slight accent, but I couldn't place it.

Cam's eyes narrowed. "Where is he, then?"

"Business," was all the man said.

"Business where, smartass?"

"He doesn't tell me these things."

I placed the accent now, and I had to smile. It was German. Fazzio had some musclebound Aryan guarding his home.

"When will he be back?" Cam pressed.

"When he is finished."

Cam looked like he was considering pistol-whipping the guy, but he held back. Instead, he looked at me and shrugged. "Then I guess we'll wait, huh?"

I belted the Terminator behind the ear with the butt end of my gun. He grunted and fell in a heap. I glanced around, looking for something to tie him up with. A lamp cord presented itself as a possibility.

When I glanced back at Cam, he was smiling.

THIRTY-THREE
Cameron

We took care of business in silence. The big bodyguard woke up midway through Bricks tying his hands behind him and I had to show him my gun and give him a warning. He sat still after that. A good soldier is used to following orders and whoever is holding the gun is the man in charge.

We left him sitting and went out in the hall where we could still see him through the open door to make sure he didn't slip his bindings, but he couldn't hear us talk.

"So after this, what is it?" I asked.

"I don't know. We can return the rental car at the airport," Bricks said hopefully.

"And ditch our guns?"

"For now."

I thought about it, but wasn't sure how I felt. I paced the hall a bit. The longer it took for Fazzio to get home, the more stressed I got. I dragged the barrel of my .44 along the wall, cutting a long gash in the wallpaper.

"I sure like this a hell of a lot more when we're getting paid for it," I said.

"I know what you mean."

"I guess maybe I'm due for a break. Whatever we decide to do."

"That extra five grand would have been nice to have..."

She looked like she'd let that one slip out without thinking, like it was something meant between her to herself. She didn't apologize though and I knew she was right. But fuck it—what's done is done.

"He's gotta have some cash around here, right?"

"He seems old school. They're more likely to keep paper money than the newer generation."

"Let's see if Hans knows anything."

We went back into the office and I stepped up in front of the German.

"Fazzio keep a safe around here?"

He looked at me deadpan, or maybe just dead. "I'm not sure."

"Want to take a guess?"

"I wouldn't know where to start."

My gun still dangled from my hand. It was heavy now, but I wanted it at the ready. I tilted it so it aimed at his kneecap. "You sure?"

The slightest crack in his granite veneer. "I don't deal with the money."

"But you might know where he keeps it?" I drew back the hammer on the Magnum. It was a deeply satisfying sound. A sphincter clenching noise like the cracking of the devil's knuckles.

He swallowed, shifted in his seat.

"Got it."

I turned and Bricks was standing against the far wall with a painting in her hand, a Boston harbor scene at sunset. On the wall in the space where the painting used to hang was a safe. The German breathed a sigh of relief.

I left him and went to Bricks. "Can you get inside?"

"Do you have a blowtorch in your pocket?"

So okay, neither one of us were a box man and there might have been a letter opener on Fazzio's desk, but we needed a crowbar and maybe a jackhammer. The safe was small, maybe twelve by twelve. And a wall mounted number can't be too deep or too heavy, but it may as well have been Fort Knox to us.

"What do we do?" I asked. "Spin the tumblers until we get lucky?"

Bricks looked at my .44. "Do you feel lucky, punk?"

I brushed off her joke but now that I was close to it, the idea of a little traveling money sounded good to me. I was regretting my choice to hand over my envelope to Tag. Perspective, I guess.

"How about you, Hans?" I turned and lifted the gun toward our German friend, marching the distance between us like a man on a mission. "You know the combo?"

He twisted his face away from the imposing barrel of my gun. "I don't know it."

Bricks went to Fazzio's desk and starting rooting around. I wished I'd asked Junior his birthday before I shot him. Or the jersey numbers of his favorite Red Sox players. I lowered my gun and joined the search. I checked the back of the painting, under the blotter on his desk, inside the humidor sitting on the side table. Nothing.

"What we need is Fazzio," I said.

Now, I've never been a praying man, but right then the door downstairs opened. It sure as hell seemed like God answered our prayers, and that he was a fan of larceny and assassinations.

Bricks closed the drawer she was searching and padded silently across the rug with her gun at the ready. I retreated to the opposite side of the door and pushed it nearly closed so he wouldn't see the German the moment he passed by the door. I looked back at Hans and held a finger to my lips, *shhhhh*.

It took another five minutes for Fazzio to start up the steps and in that time we heard two voices—his and a young girl. I knew she was young by the way she laughed at every stupid thing he said. She had that sorority girl giggle and it had the speed of someone on coke, which I guessed was the only way a young girl like that could take a night out with an aging don like Fazzio. What girls wouldn't do for a diamond bracelet or hell, these days, for a new iPhone.

He pushed open the door with one hand, the other around his neck loosening a tie. He froze when he saw—in rapid succession—the tied-up German, Bricks with a gun on him and me with my gun and a smile.

"You," he said.

"Me," I answered.

"Call her up here," Bricks said. Always on task.

Without taking his eyes off me, Fazzio turned his head to the open door. "Gina! Come here, honey."

We all stood still as Gina padded up the steps in her bare feet, the evening's heels already kicked off.

"What is it—?"

Bricks grabbed her by the hair and put the gun to her temple. To Gina's credit, she didn't scream. She whimpered and tried to swallow sobs, but she stayed as calm as anyone could expect. Fazzio kept his cool too. He lifted his hands in a token gesture to surrender. The wound I'd given him on his cheek had healed but still had a nasty look to it. He eyed me with an expression equal parts tired and enraged.

"You killed my son."

I held his eye: steady, strong. "I did."

"It's a funny business," he said, then added a sigh like he knew this day would come. "You kill one of ours so we figure we gotta kill you. Now you've killed my son and by rights I should have your head, but here we are, with you about to go one up on me. This game is about to end with an uneven score."

"If not, the game goes on forever."

"Doesn't it anyway?" he said.

I really didn't want philosophy right then and I hated how right he was. I also didn't want another goddamn bloodbath. The German and the girl could walk away from this unharmed if they'd let it play out and realize they weren't the targets.

"Hey, asshole," Bricks said. "Shut up already."

On task. Always on task.

"You must be Bricks," he said.

"Yeah, and I'm even harder to kill than he is." She pointed at me with her gun. Gina let out a small whimper.

"Why not let the girl go?" Fazzio said.

"We will. When it's done."

Fazzio looked at Bricks, then me. "Well, then...what are we waiting for?"

I stuffed the revolver in my back pocket and grabbed Fazzio by the lapels. I pushed him toward the window. The German started struggling against his restraints. Gina let loose with the tears she'd been holding in.

Fazzio had a gut on him, he wasn't a small man. Pushing him backward knocked him off balance and I ended up carrying him the last few steps before I slammed him into the window frame. The window was still open from when me and Bricks came in and I returned the favor to Fazzio for the way he'd hung me out a window when we first met.

The German got a hand or a foot loose, something I could only see as movement out of my peripheral vision. Bricks stepped up to him, Gina in tow by the hair, and shot the man through the foot. He yelled out, but stayed in his seat.

I pushed Fazzio out through the window, holding tight to his jacket front.

"How do you like it?"

I saw the first real fear in his face. He held on to my wrists and stole glances below him to the alley where the ladder lay like broken bones. This wasn't as high up as the window he held me out of, but it was enough to put the scare into him.

Gina's wailing got louder and I heard Bricks yell, "You want me to shoot you too? Is that what you want? Then shut the fuck up."

"I want you to know," I said to him. "You started this."

I tried to summon all my anger. The anger at being lured up to Boston, at being held in a room and made to think I was going to die at any minute. For being cut and beaten and shot at. For having my Aunt Ruby killed and cousin thrown in jail and another cousin broken.

Funny thing was, it wasn't enough. Even all that added up didn't make me want to end Fazzio's life in as much pain as I could think of. I thought that's what I'd come here for, but I was wrong. All the satisfaction I wanted could have been achieved with a sniper rifle from a half mile away. I wanted him gone so he couldn't follow us. I wanted to be left alone, that's all.

"Cam, let's hurry up," Bricks said. She was right. I was dragging this out on the verge of another Slaughterhouse special. Not this time.

I pulled him back in the room, let him slump to the floor.

"Open the safe," I said.

Fazzio looked up at me, heavy breathing and with a twitchy eye. "The safe?"

I pointed to the wall. "The safe. Open it."

The German tried to defend his honor. "I didn't tell them anything."

I drew the .44 and pointed the way with the barrel. "Now," I said.

Fazzio first got on all fours and crawled a few feet, then slowly got to his feet, showing every long week of his age.

"If he gives you money, you'll let us go?" Gina asked.

"I'll let you go if you don't say another fucking word," Bricks said. She flung Gina by her hair over to the German. Gina fell on top of him, re-aggravating his foot injury. He screamed and she started crying again, the two of them in a pile.

Fazzio spun the tumbler on the wall safe and in three turns it opened.

"Hand it over," I said.

He took out five stacks of neatly wrapped cash. I didn't count how much, but in the thousands. There were some other papers in there but we both knew I didn't care about them so he left them and I didn't ask.

"You started this," I said again.

Fazzio leaned against the wall beside the open safe. "Just make it quick. Please, make it quick."

I shot him in the forehead. Quick.

My pockets full with the money, I turned to Bricks who stood over our two captives. I wanted to feel a sense of relief, like a weight had been lifted. I wanted to feel free and happy with the new cash in my pocket. I didn't feel any of that. And right then I knew I never would. That's not what this life brings you. And even if I never pulled a trigger again, the way I felt right then was deep in the marrow of my bones. I'd never be truly free. There would always be a shadow at my back.

THIRTY-FOUR
Bricks

The look on Cam's face immediately after Fazzio slumped to the ground was one I'd never seen on him before. I couldn't quite pin it down, either, but one thing was clear. He'd turned some kind of corner. I didn't have time right then to figure out any more than that. There was work to be done.

"Omigod, omigod, omigaaaaaaaaaaaaawd," blubbered Gina. Her voice rose an octave with each exclamation, and the volume was going up, too. The German remained silent, gritting his teeth against the pain in his foot. He stared at me with an odd mixture of hopeless defiance.

"Your call," Cam said quietly. His expression had softened some, but the strange resolve remained.

Gina and the German. Christ, it sounded like a failed TV sitcom pilot. The idiot girlfriend and the honorable bodyguard. Laugh at their half-hour hijinks. What a pair.

"The best move is to kill them," I said, my voice cold. "No witnesses."

"Noooo!" Gina wailed.

I pointed the gun at her. "I hear another peep come out of your cock garage, and that is exactly what I'm going to do."

She clamped her mouth shut.

I looked at Cam, and his expression damn near broke my heart. He didn't want to kill these two, I could tell. He knew it was the smart play, and he'd follow my lead if I went that way, but it was plain to me that it was the last thing he wanted to do.

I thought about it for another ten seconds. I ran out the scenarios in my head, and I made a decision.

"You," I said to the German. "Hans."

"Kasper," he said. "Mein name ist Kasper."

I didn't need to speak German to get what he said. Or what he was doing. Humanizing yourself is one of the best defenses against being killed when you're a hostage. That's why terrorists put a bag over the heads of their prisoners. Because no matter how hard you are, there is something very innate in each of us that makes killing another human being difficult. That's a strange realization for someone in my line of work to make, but it was one I'd become comfortable with. I'd rationalized that I only killed people in the life, people who had it coming. Maybe true, but it was still killing. And while I hadn't lost my nerve for it, the look on Cam's face certainly made me lose any desire to do any more of it today.

"Personally, I don't give a fuck if your name is Adolf," I told Kasper, maintaining my cold exterior. "What I care about is that you and sugar tits here can keep a story straight."

He digested what I'd just said, then nodded. "I can."

I waved the barrel of my gun at Gina, who still gulping sobs. "What about her?"

He considered. I didn't like that he had to think about it. Finally, he said, "I think so, yes."

I turned my attention to Gina. "He thinks so. What do you think, Gina?"

She nodded frantically, then opened her mouth to assure me some more.

I held up my hand to stop her. "No, see you're about to do what exactly I don't want you to do. Talk. Get it?"

She hesitated, then nodded again. She let out a whiny "mmmm-hhhmmm" to go with it.

"Okay," I said. "So the story you tell the cops and anyone else who asks is that a couple of Italians in track suits busted in here. They tied you up," I pointed to Kasper, "and waited for Fazzio to come home. And then it went down just like this did. He opened the safe, the gavone shot him in the head, and ba-da-boom, ba-da-bing, they left with the cash." I eyed both of them. "Got it?

Gina bobbed her head, but Kasper didn't reply right away. Then he asked, "When did they shoot my foot, these Italians?"

I thought about it. "While they were waiting for Fazzio. To get you to talk. You didn't."

"Did I know these men?"

I shook my head. "For the cops, definitely not. They'll expect nothing less. For the family?" I shrugged. "You want to blame this on some dicks from Providence, or even the city, go ahead. But not a whisper about us. This thing with us is over."

Kasper didn't have to think about it for long. He nodded once briskly. "Ist gut."

"You give us fifteen minutes, and then you can call whoever you like," I told him. "Because it won't matter. We are going to be long gone. Forever."

Once we got out of the warren of residential streets in Fazzio's neighborhood and hit an arterial, I got us on a freeway with no trouble. I don't know if Kasper actually waited fifteen minutes to call anyone, but if he did, Cam and I were already westbound at five over the speed limit by the time he let his fingers do the walking.

We rode in silence for the better part of an hour. I figured I'd let the silence sit for a while longer if he wanted, but I'd have to break it sooner or later to make sure he was all right with my plan. If he was, great. If he wasn't, I'd have to take an exit and drop him at a bus station.

He lasted another five minutes. Then he said, "Thanks."

"For what?"

"For coming to Boston." He was quiet for another minute or so, then added, "And for not killing those two."

"No problem."

"I know it was the smart move to shoot them, too. I just—"

"No problem," I repeated.

A small smile touched the corner of his mouth. Then he chuckled a little, and the smile grew.

"What's so goddamn funny?"

"Please come to Boston...," he half sang, "for some revenge."

I smiled, and joined in. "I got shot up by Fazzio and I need some help."

He laughed out loud. "Yeah, that doesn't work. And your voice is horrible. Keep your day job."

"My day job is pretty much in the rearview mirror."

He thought about that. "Yeah, maybe. But can I ask you a question?"

"Go ahead."

"What else are you gonna do? What else am I gonna do?"

"I don't know. I'm not much good at anything else."

"Me neither."

"I don't know that I really want to do anything else."

"Me neither."

I gave him a quick glance. "A moment ago, you were tired of it all. Now you can't walk away?"

He shrugged. "I'm a complicated man."

"Complicated, maybe. Man?" I made an unsure sound.

He snorted. "Always busting balls, Bricks." He took a deep breath and let it out in a long sigh. Then he said, "I guess I just want to make sure that they always deserve what they get. Can we do that, and still do this job?"

"I've been telling myself yes for years now."

"Is it working?"

"Not great, but I get by."

"Can I ask another question?"

"Can I stop you?" I thought he might ask how much I thought we got out of Fazzio's safe, but he asked the more obvious question instead.

"Where the fuck we going?"

"West," I said. "Way west." I thought about it another moment, and added, "I think we'll know where when we get there."

He nodded his head in agreement. "And then what?"

"Exactly," I answered. "And then what."

He didn't answer. He didn't have to. Instead, he settled into his seat, leaned his head against the window, and went to sleep. That settled it.

And me? I kept the car on the road, between the lines, hurtling westward.

ABOUT THE AUTHORS

Eric Beetner is the author of more than a dozen novels including *Rumrunners* and its sequel *Leadfoot*, *The Devil Doesn't Want Me* and its sequel *When The Devil Comes To Call*, *Dig Two Graves*, *Run For The Money*, and *The Year I Died Seven Times*. His award-winning stories have appeared in over twenty anthologies including *Unloaded: Crime Writers Writing Without Guns*, which he created and edited. He is co-author (with JB Kohl) of *One Too Many Blows To The Head*, *Borrowed Trouble* and *Over Their Heads* and co-wrote *The Backlist* and *The Short List* with author Frank Zafiro. He lives in Los Angeles where he co-hosts the Noir At The Bar reading series. For more visit http://www.ericbeetner.com/.

Frank was a police officer in Spokane, Washington, from 1993 to 2013. He retired as a captain. He is the author of numerous crime novels, including River City novels and the Stefan Kopriva series. This is his second novel with Eric Beetner. In addition to writing, Frank teaches leadership and other law enforcement topics to police officers and college students alike. He is an avid hockey fan and a tortured guitarist. He lives in Chattaroy, Washington, with his wife and youngest son. You can keep up with Frank at http://frankzafiro.com.

OTHER TITLES FROM DOWN AND OUT BOOKS

See www.DownAndOutBooks.com for complete list

By J.L. Abramo
Catching Water in a Net
Clutching at Straws
Counting to Infinity
Gravesend
Chasing Charlie Chan
Circling the Runway
Brooklyn Justice

By Trey R. Barker
2,000 Miles to Open Road
Road Gig: A Novella
Exit Blood
Death is Not Forever
No Harder Prison

By Richard Barre
The Innocents
Bearing Secrets
Christmas Stories
The Ghosts of Morning
Blackheart Highway
Burning Moon
Echo Bay
Lost

By Eric Beetner (editor)
Unloaded

By Eric Beetner and JB Kohl
Over Their Heads

By Eric Beetner and Frank Scalise
The Backlist
The Short List

By G.J. Brown
Falling

By Rob Brunet
Stinking Rich

By Dana Cameron (editor)
Murder at the Beach: Bouchercon Anthology 2014

By Mark Coggins
No Hard Feelings

By Tom Crowley
Vipers Tail
Murder in the Slaughterhouse

By Frank De Blase
Pine Box for a Pin-Up
Busted Valentines and Other Dark Delights
A Cougar's Kiss

By Les Edgerton
The Genuine, Imitation, Plastic Kidnapping

By A.C. Frieden
Tranquility Denied
The Serpent's Game
The Pyongyang Option (*)

By Jack Getze
Big Numbers
Big Money
Big Mojo
Big Shoes

(*)—Coming Soon

OTHER TITLES FROM DOWN AND OUT BOOKS

See www.DownAndOutBooks.com for complete list

By Richard Godwin
Wrong Crowd
Buffalo and Sour Mash (*)

By William Hastings (editor)
Stray Dogs: Writing from the Other America

By Jeffery Hess
Beachhead

By Matt Hilton
No Going Back
Rules of Honor
The Lawless Kind
The Devil's Anvil

By David Housewright
Finders Keepers
Full House

By Jerry Kennealy
Screen Test

By S.W. Lauden
Crosswise

By Terrence McCauley
The Devil Dogs of Belleau Wood

By Bill Moody
Czechmate
The Man in Red Square
Solo Hand
The Death of a Tenor Man
The Sound of the Trumpet
Bird Lives!

By Gary Phillips
The Perpetrators
Scoundrels (Editor)
Treacherous
3 the Hard Way

By Tom Pitts
Hustle

By Robert J. Randisi
Upon My Soul
Souls of the Dead
Envy the Dead (*)

By Ryan Sayles
The Subtle Art of Brutality
Warpath
Swansongs Always Begin as Love Songs (*)

By John Shepphird
The Shill
Kill the Shill
Beware the Shill (*)

By Ian Thurman
Grand Trunk and Shearer (*)

James R. Tuck (editor)
Mama Tried: vol. 1

By Lono Waiwaiole
Wiley's Lament
Wiley's Shuffle
Wiley's Refrain
Dark Paradise
Leon's Legacy (*)

(*)—Coming Soon

33715855R00150

Made in the USA
Middletown, DE
24 July 2016